COLLECTION OF SHORT STORIES

BY

IFTEKHAR JALIL BAIG

Become
Shakespeare
.com

First Published in 2020 by

Becomeshakespeare.com

One Point Six Technologies Pvt. Ltd.
119-123, 1st Floor, Building J2, B - Wing,
Wadala Truck Terminal, Wadala East,
Mumbai 400022, Maharashtra, INDIA
T: +91 8080226699

ISBN - 978-81-948041-0-9

Dedicated to my father

Foreword

This collage of chapters ,some are my personal opinion and beliefs,some are my vivid imaginations run wild while other are results of my experiences.

The stories are mostly devoid of time and space localization,they could be anywhere and timeless.

Nomemenclature of persons and place are intentionally lacking.

Expecting the audience to extrapolate,put in practice and also enjoy.

Contents

Contents

The Burial

I was twelve then, seems to me ages have passed, I feel now almost twelve again just the thought I am going to think of that time, I was mostly unnoticed at that time.

I remember fondly how I used to come back hopping from school to the very same house of my grandparents, my parents died in an accident at an age when with best of piercing thought it is impossible to recollect the faces. I see the album and try very very hard to think that I can at least place this image to the real persons, just once I want to see the real profile of my parents but it is always an impossible task I just cannot glimpse.

In my dreams these very photograph of the album come to me never the real image I want to see.

Coming from school at such a time and getting the first glimpse of my grandparents house always filled me with joy. No it was not much of a grand scale house, neither very beautiful architectured at that.

It was one of those little houses that go almost unnoticed by anyone, not much of a garden either, a small patch of land on its side seemed as all luxury of a garden possible, it was also a favorite haunt of my grandpa with his daily habit of reading in the evening under the shade of the lovely tree. There was as much space only for one tree possible in the small area. He would from almost five till ten not change his routine of devouring a book in that favorite spot of his which never changed until passing of the seasons or with the passage of years and decade.

My fancy for that house was the little room with a turret like roof, that was my room, it had two windows a large window opening to the intrusion of branches which always seemed to frenzy inside the room, in an unabashedly shamelessness that was always noticed when you opened the window.

My room had an almirah one that was curtained not one of the famous names attached but had an age almost the same as my grandpa. It was not one could pass by in an antique dealer shop every day, my bed was on the contrary beddings only, and there was just enough space for a study table and chair.

The moment I returned from school I would not waste a minute came rain or any other work of the day, it was always to rush and open my window and sit for some time doing nothing, a habit almost permanent.

This was to go on, and did I mention I did all which a twelve year old would do, play with children in the afternoon, take a nap, tease my grandma with a regular punctuality.

I was happy in the mundane routined way of my life but that was not to be, some thing was to happen which would take away all my pleasure away no longer would I be happy if that was what I was earlier ever in my childhood. Now that I am old I only remember but no longer have similar pangs as in my childhood.

I was coming back from school one afternoon with the sun being in somber mood word was behind the clouds as if punctuality itself before it started in a fit of frenzy to scorch the earth. The leaves came singing along with the gentle wind, I was in my regular stick when I saw a funeral procession pass by in the by lane, the cemetery was not very far from the place I was standing, barely half a kilometer away, I have heard of deaths so far, my grandpa went for the funeral of the neighbors, but I was never as much as near to the corpse or the procession. I somehow under my boyish exterior, the growing man worked to explore this possibility of discovering this new experience.

I crossed the road and in a slow tread was limping behind the twenty odd people who were ahead of me. I walked slowly behind watching the faces of other, some were noticeably sad others sad with an almost grim face and some were doing this as a routine, they had to be because members counted in there matters I suppose.

It was with this thought of looking at faces I was occupied and knew not exactly how long it took but I was besides the burial rite.

The usual preparation of the farewell, the usual customs and the usual procedure were to follow.

It was with this preoccupation of mind I was involved when I happened to glance at the opposite end not few yards away was a young girl, she had her one hand on the tombstone and the other one by the lowest branch of the nearest tree, it must have been a very common sight in the cemetery I suppose, the canvas this is was probably painted every day by someone or the other.

Yes, I was now no longer with the strangers funeral which till now I was following intently step by step experiencing this new found experience of mine. I was now with that girl completely, in spirit at least.

Yes she was beautiful, her face was sober yet with no outward expression of grief, the eyes wave intent on the occupant of the grave. There was as if a conversation taking place which appeared that somehow only the sounds were absent, this was a long conversation the girl seemed to be questioning then a pause sometimes brief and sometimes long, the pauses were the unheard answers I suppose there would be an occasional smile which would soon turn to that sobriety again, there would be an occasional show of anguish then again that sobriety.

I now moved a few yards away from the service in which I was present to another tombstone.

In my confusion at the loneliness of the place and along with that the thought that I would be noticed by the girl as somewhat spying on her.

I tried to get her best view yet wanted to conceal somewhere, I wanted to notice her in all her actions it was very difficult to take away myself from that girl, the bond which I had established with that girl was intense. It was no to be broken by any means.

I shuddered at the very thought that this canvas in front of me would be bereft of that girl in a few moment of time, how long not some that few minutes. I prayed that this girl would be there for an hour, I wanted to see her, watch all her steps, all her actions, all her beauty.

Her hands almost sparkled in the light, her hand with the fingers framed a harmonious sight, the finger on the tombstone could almost create music by tapping on the tombstone, she had all the grace.

Who was the occupant, why would I bother, should I, yet her features suggested it was someone she had liked immensely, who probably mother, father a close friend I suppose.

It would never occur to me then it could be her lover or beloved, not that other twelve years had no idea of that, for me it was an alien thought then, you could say I was slow in my development, my milestones had not achieved that stage.

I noticed her low neck dress, the clefts riveted my attention, I was shall I say spellbound, I was noticing her beautiful long neck that was holding her head high in an almost majestic manner, she was beautiful. Her eyes had a language of her own. I was there standing, she was there standing, it was as if I was saying something to her not bothered whether she replied or not.

Then her communication with the occupant must have stopped she was still, her still and sober, no anguish remained as such as long as she stood there, I found myself an emotion I cannot describe, it is almost undescribable , I wanted to be towards her feel her, hold her hands.

I level my best of imagination to assure she was by me, her physical self with me, I held my other hand and tried to experience her, I felt frustrated as no amount of my imagination was sufficient to give me the feeling I was holding her hands. I walked a few yards away from where I was not fearing that now she might notice me I had a courage because in my mind I was sure that I have had enough conversation with her to be called one of her acquaintence.

I stood there just few meter away from her she raised her head towards me and the way she would look at a boy and glanced her view away just as one would look at a passing stray dog and take the glance away. I felt hurt. She had not reciprocated all my fond gesture to her.

surely I deserved to be seen for longer than she glanced. Now, after a moment I composed myself and started my "experience" of this young girl with all intent.

I was now not bothered if she would notice my presence. I simply went on looking at her, unabashedly ,shamelessly , I wanted her to remain these for hours, I wanted her to be there everyday for hours.

She was not bothered of me and continued her stay there, probably she was not bothered because I stood where it was impossible for her not to notice me, yet she took no notice. She was at her contemplation quiet, still. Then with slow head she turned was walking towards the gate. The gate was not a long walk, I was shattered I slowly walked behind her she was aware of me walking behind, yet she did not turn her back. I was noticing her strides and at the gate she turned to the road which goes opposite to my house.

With all my eagerness to follow her I somewhat stood back the road before it turned was not long, I stood there and watched her swifting through the road to the other end. She was there no more.I stood by the gate for almost an hour thinking about her over and over again. She was simply a delight.

I then slowly walked back to where she had stood, I noticed her footsteps eagerly delighting myself with eyes closed that she was still standing here. I might have stood there for sometime with a heavy heart I started moving towards the gate.

Again I watched the road she had stepped on to and then I moved in the direction of my home in a few minutes I was home, I opened my window and the shameless branches intruded my room I sat in my chair, no one was home.

I sat there for a very long time thinking of her all the time. The haunting thought of her would not leave me. It was not long that time swiftly ran, even with the restrain of my faculties.

It was night and the night was restless as ever it could be, I was not in my person any more, I wanted to willfully dream of her, I wanted her to be in my dreams unconsciously. But that would not be. I was awake the whole night.

I picked up my colour box and thinking myself some painter of great talent tried to recreate the real canvas I have seen of her by the tree and the tombstone.

It was impossible, what was made was what looked like a girl by a tree. It was morning, grandma came to wake me who had not slept a wink, still discipline ruled school it had to be.

I went to school, not at all with the teachers that day I was away in the cemetery. No sooner than the school was over I was over to the cemetery. I stood where she had stood, that faceless tombstone showed no clue, I was searching nothing, I did not want to know where she lived, I just wanted to be where she was, it was delightful feeling. Day after day it was the same a little late from school. I was there where she was.

With time first my devotion decreased then then it would be weekly, finally it just got over. I would never be there

I remember how I would ponder there, will she come now, no earlier it was not anticipating her visit that I would go, just the thought that she was there would make me go there. I have after that never gone there, I live in some other city, pretty far from that place, I am well placed, life I wanted to know whose grave it was, but was surprising impossible to know, I have never ever seen her again nor have I further passion to go after her. Yet for some reason, I have changed houses, I have changed furniture I have changed a lot of my belongings, thrown away a lot of junk, many childhood remembrances were willfully thrown away, I have also discarded a lot of my family heirlooms ,for want and space and ease of what a travelling man desires.

Still in my trunk full of books, some where rolled up in the corner is the painting all frayed at side, changed colour with age, ugly to the aesthetic eye lies that very same painting done when I was twelve. I never gather enough courage to throw that away.

A Love story

It was the remotest part of earth, an almost endless vast icy plateau led to undending ranges, in between numerous cliffs, hills, ice capped at the summit.

In this vast barren land there was an inhabitation clustered around a little town, a small monastery, a rest house for the occasional trekker who might reach there.

It was shut to the outside world to the extreme, he was the son of the owner of the rest house.

He was said by the residents to be the most handsome, beautiful and indeed he was.

If shown to the outside world he would perhaps be the steal of the catwalk.

He was splendidly handsome.

At twenty, carefree, he knew the occasional passerby crossing would pay enough to keep him happy for rest of his life.

Mother had died, he was alone with his father.

He was respected but he did not find others in league with him.

Chance.

The daughter of the steel giant, without which it is safely said the world would not be the same, was trekking and was passing this area.

It was her fancy at nineteen to these far flung remote places that had made it possible.

She had travelled alone so far, here too she was travelling alone.

She was an unsaid princess.

She was beautiful, almost fairy tale.

It turned out that soon she was face to face with this person in the resthouse.

She had seen the world, yet there was an attractive charm of this person, not yet found in others by her.

He spoke her language with difficulty, yet understandable.

She was his guest, a week she would stay here, this place had caught her imagination to almost an insane excess.

The solitude, the splendour, all appealed to her.

Yes, it was to be for a week.

He led her to her room, small talk ensued.

They parted.

She was forgotten.

Next morning, she wanted to go around, he was called, his vehicle would take her around, he was to be her guide.

It was a mere business proposal.

The day moved with surprisingly slow pace, in these remote places time stands still, hours become days. she was happy with all she saw.

One never knows when she turned to see him, one never knows that one who had seen the world, one who could get anything by purchasing, would fix her attention to him.

He was not much of a talker, no education, neither experience to be shared he had never left this town.

What was it then, yes he was handsome but many more handsome than him would die to be at her company.

One can never conjecture how the machinery of love works, she was dying to be with him.

He was ignorant, but not inasmuch, he understood.

They returned to the room it was an almost unimaginable frenzy, they were united.

Words need not be exchanged, was to be that way.

It was lust or love.

They were not bothered, one too ignorant and the other not bothered.

They were content.

He was now in a similar mood, all for her.

Morning. They talked, their disparities got explained. he was now ashamed of his actions.

Slowly they were explaining to each other, sometimes the futilities of such a relationship, sometimes consolidating their position.

Time moved slowly, she was here for a week and then it would be over, he thought.

Not her, it was to be with him all her life.

Details were to be worked out at a later stage.

An unending love arose between them, forgetting his humble origin, he too realised his love for her, at least in this aspect he was in equal grounds with her.

Days and nights were to vanish now with rapidity. Both wanted time to stand still, yet time would now have wings.

On the seventh morning, after an endless untiring union, they were walking, they walked the whole day sharing love and affection till they reached the precipice, from there you could see hundreds of meters below the the endless icy plateau.

They embraced, kissed and no one knows both of them had not discussed this, both had not planned this.

They moved closer to the edge and holding each other, eyes talked, they nodded, with a tear in her eye and a smile in his face they both took a leap.

A close shave

I was reading a very funny book, role of barbers in the medieval world, quite surprised both in the east and the west the barbers had been quite instrumental in making successful court intrigues in changing monarch in rebellions and what not, I was figuring the absence of Africa and the ancient world, it would not have been surprising that they had their say then as well.

Anyway no one except the queen consort was ever close to the king. This reading gave me a desire for a haircut. I went to my favourite. A group of ten were sitting with their 'favourite' hair dresser in the men's parlour.

When I sat three were leaving.

Besides me the headline of the day was being discussed in greatest detail, it appeared to me they were not happy with the government's foreign policy of invasion about to take place.

"No, the timing is right, we have suffered enough of diplomatic insults, a lot of harassment, just read the papers of past fifty years, that border has shown enough reasons said the fat chap.

"We should be stern with them now, show them we cannot keep quiet anymore."

"What about the humanitarian grounds" said the barber in the corner.

"What humanitarian grounds it is insulting for us to keep quiet in our "House", in their diplomatic arena and in the international forms"

"War is old fashioned, out dated" said one barber.

"Yes" the barbers were agreed on not having a war.

"I quiet agree with the war" said I we have taken quietly for long under this facade of various grounds our inability to retaliate."

The barbers were visibly angry, it was in their grounds with cut threat razors that was I saying against them. They were not happy at all, debate, reasons they would perhaps take in with ease but a point blank decision they will not tolerate.

I didn't know if you have ever visited these in midst of a serious conversation, they are somewhat not much bothered of clientele, their profession is reasonably in favour of them rather the clientele. In demand and supply there are really in shortage these days.

It is never popular to live without them ever in any millenium.

They are in complete control, perhaps if you are annoyed with them, somehow you will have to return to them.

I was now their prime target in this discussion. There was innumerable cases, points they cited, they were over the years quite in control with all the information.

If you ever said something not substantial they would quote the exact figures and the picture of the happening.

Somehow all the customers were involved in this discussion.

There was a heated argument.

Somehow deep within I felt it was better other days when the argument and discussion raged over some other topics.

Now this was really upsetting to me.

The place had become outrageous.

I tried to divert the topic to some latest release of movies and music.

"It is people like you, who don't have a spine, that our great nation has crumbled, we could be superpower but for people like you" said an angry customer.

I kept quiet, it was not my day.

The consensus was reached that "Peace is better alternative to war at any cost."

Noticeably the only silent customer in the entire proceeding was the person who spoke finally "there will be a further high level meeting to review the situation." It was a face one does not easily forget, it was Minister for foreign affairs.

The barbers continued at their own pace of work hardly noticing anything.

I along with other customers were looking quite full of awe at his presence. We were truly surprised unable to say anything.

While I was returning home I drew a parallel with my book I was reading, who knows what course of action the government will take.

Time changes, ages change, an era changes its fashion its way of life, something does not change it remains in some traces the same as it was.

Well I suppose this is life again.

The last breath

He was thirty, handsome, broad shouldered, calm, quiet good humoured and an established person of his profession namely a manager, manager of one of the franchised global financial giants we all know of.

He was well paid by any standards, he had a large house in the suburbia and had all modern amenities you and I can think of which would supposedly keep any one happy in the world.

He was not married, but had his parents living in the nearby city, his extended family was a large one,not of the persons we knew who are with very limited number of family members.

Though limited in his social life, yet he had a large number of acquaintances, everyone of them would probably help him when he needed their help most.

A close circle of friends who would regularly meet him or he would be invited.

His social calendar would show he was a respectable member of cites largest club, he was infrequent gambler a keen eye with the horses made him frequent the race course from time to time. His engagements at parties showed he was not one averse to meeting a large gathering of public.

To date he was not steady with anyone, yet he was not known not to mix with members of the opposite sex.

Overall, the acquaintances often talked of him with respect, wished to know him further, liked his company the reciprocation showed he was a respectable member liked by the society. This was all till this October, till now this very practical cool and good temperament person who had seen little ups and downs of life was not altogether frenzied or uprooted ever from his depths..

He was extremely fond of one of his maternal uncle's son's wife. A great fondness an extreme brotherly affection for this girl had evolved in him ever since by way of marriage she had come into the family five years back. Day by day fondness and love increased an increasing frequency of visits were to ensue.

The rest of the world were equally balanced by her company alone to him, love takes strange form it was similar with this man. There was a fair balance though in the relationship. One could suppose a different possessiveness in different relationship is possible. He was attached excessively to her, although as we have seen till now this has not altered his attachments with others nor has narrowed his activities in other sphere of life.

October, this changed, in a day to day happening a common place thing took place, she met with an accident on the roadside, there was barely time enough to reach the hospital and she died. She died but this was to lead our man into something unimaginable.

He attended the funeral, continued the day's work and returned home.

It was five in the afternoon. He knew what he would do, he would end his life. In no time a large kitchen knife sharp enough to cause sure death was placed in front of the table.

He was thinking of her, no portrait of her was placed on the table. His heart had her image, he knew that seeing a part portrait would not change his mind nor it would give him comfort it was his mental image of that girl that assisted him all the while.

Carefully he thought of his life, he knew he would end it all this night, he would not see the next morning, he thought of mama who was ever so precious to him, his joy of life, all he wanted in life was to make her happy, she would not be happy. She would probably grieve most probably forever, she was young still and would have a life full of suffering. She would suffer everyday, every hour his loss, though they met infrequently, she would cherish his company, talk of him with others for hours she loved him dearly, mama would miss him to the utmost. No, no, no, nothing will change his mind.

He was simply trying to recollect everything how she was by him when he had a nightmare, how she was rebuking him with his first drink, how she stopped him from his various faults of the world he had picked.

He remembered the vacation together they had gone and were discussing almost everything, mama always knew what he did not, she was almost superior to others.

His thought went to the last visit, he had promised her some expensive jewellery. No, there was no point in purchasing and leaving it for her.

Daddy came next, they were almost friends, they shared all the secrets, they comforted each other, life was not always pleasant for both of them.

Sometimes or the other, each needed the shoulder of other, consolation worked both ways, they were very fond of each other.

Every moment of togetherness had some good feelings. A range of emotions shared by both of them, there was millions of thought of moments shared. Too long to be recollected, all were precious too precious what would he feel, he would never understand why he had done this. He would be grieve for the rest of his life. He was not the person who shared this excessive love he had for this girl. Daddy was smart but he was to leave daddy with a big question mark, probably daddy one day would be first to understand why he did it but for long many year he would be confused, bewildered, unable to guess, and yes would never forget him. Daddy's pride he has been his father pride over the years, was he not an achiever a very good achievement in life he had done by daddy's standard. Daddy was looking forward for far more victories in his life.

Waiting to applaud him at all steps, pat him for all the achievements daddy needed nothing, but every visit for daddy would mean he buying expensive gifts, always a statement so daddy feels happier.

Probably daddy after him would make one room a museum for him, keeping things of his together, and remembering him always, entering that place everyday to feel him even in his absence.

He knew he was being harsh to daddy but life has lost its purpose.

He had a very large extended family, all would meet yearly for some reason or the other, together they would share moments of happiness compressed in days what one would cherish for years. He thought of all the mail he had done to them in nearing days. He thought of their mail he had received they were all precious part of his life. All of them would accuse him of a deciet, all would never forgive him, they would probably all gather and grieve not only the moment but remember forever.

He recollected one by one their association with him, their fondness for him, their words, his words all were coming back in this last hour which he himself had bestowed on himself.

No not ever for all the nest it was for her he was to end his life he would have nothing else he had decided.

They all were fond of him, to everyone for something special aspect of his life he was varied in approach to life. All had a bond with him in some way or the other. He was what one can say the jewel in the crown.

No he had no hatred received from any one of his extended family, they all loved him, he was precious to all of them, he was going to be missed by them.

The worse part they will all wonder for the rest of their lives why he did this, they would all think he had no right to cheat them like this. Some would say "not in this way" that he had ended himself.

His life was precious to one and all. They were all supportive to him, they would question why he did not take their support in his greatest hour of need.

All of them would be shattered.

All of them would have a question to mark.

All of them would never forgive themselves.

All of them would never forgive him.

He was not here to think of them and pause to stop himself from this maniacal action, he was just recollecting his life before the thread of life left his body.

He thought of all his family members their cities, their houses, ever their pets who he knew them all by their first name.

He was trying to forgive out what each of them would be doing now, he made mental image of everyone imagining what they were doing now.

Even imagining what their pets would be doing. He was now very calm, he was not at all frenzied.

He had the family album, but he would not see it mental image was better.

Each relationship he shared was precious for either parties, each relationship was invaluable, he was not trying to alter his plans it was just that he was lovingly recollecting his life.

It was for her he was giving up his life, cheating others, destroying others, yet he was not to change his mind, he was decided. It had to be done. It needed to be done, it was to be done tonight just for her.

Then came his friends, he named them,imagined them his past relationships with them his parents relationship with them, he imagined what they would be doing now, also the pets.

He was very fond of them, they were fond of him.

It was going to be a setback for them. They all wanted him to succeed, reach whenever he wanted to be.

Now it would be difficult for him he was trying to reconcile to the fact that they would probably forget him in weeks this absence would probably be not noticed in the near future he would probably be a thing of past sooner than can be imagined. Who has the time.

But no they might blame themselves too, were they not to help him when he needed them, was this not the time to help him, he must have felt alone, he must have felt extremely distrustful of others since he confided in no one and passed his life away like this.

They would all curse themselves, for not supporting him in time when he needed them most.

He remembered all their moments, it raced the activities together, the music together, the gaiety together, the vacations together, the parties together everything came to his mind.

But no it was for her he was decided, he would do it, nothing can possibly change his mind. His friends had all helped him now he would be leaving them with a big question mark.

Everyone else he knew in passing of sphere of life for people small to people larger than life's image, all came together.

All gathered as if it's life last salute to him. It was his mental image of them yet it was true they were all saluting his acquaintance.

He would not leave them without some sorrow. In some way he's life had touched them. They were not animals they would miss him.

He thought of all the pets he had over the years their dead and alive.

He was thinking of live in the whole. His profession, he started with his office the staff, no tomorrow an acting manager would take change work would continue yet he was going to be remembered if only in way of a theatrical tribute. He could see that happening in front of his eyes. His eyes moistened.

He gave a glance to his personal wealth, probably daddy would do best with what he owned.

He closed his eyes and thought of all the rooms the furnitures the whole content of the house, he was lovingly remembering piece by piece how he had shaped this house.

He thought of neighbours, whom he had talked, who have talked to him, who have seen him only, where he had only seen it went on like a great movie running in front of him. He was thinking of everything.

The last purchase he made was the grocery he even remembered that, not to mention, his collision today with an old man who had firmly rebuked him.

He was going back in time, his life now, his school, the forgotten school friends, they loved him, hated him, he hated them, loved them, it was unfolding, his recurrent fall and injuring his knee, probably bore an eternal graze on the knee cap, it was running and changing, it was mocking teachers, scolding, the punishments. The adoration all received with passage of time, he had never thought that the school building would be in front of him, how he would like to touch its windows the desks again. He could go to see it and postpone his plans yet he was decided for that "girl" he would have to leave this world.

There was no time to open the desk and see the childhood photographs, all mental images were sufficient.

It would have to continue his mind raced to the university, all sorts of activities, all kinds of people, he was stopping at nothing, life was kind to him all throughout.

As a mark of respect to life all were to be recollected, they would all have to be renewed.

His mind raced to his first job, the second and then this job, the people, even some good customers were now coming in his mind. It was continuing, everything was continuing. He was stopping at nothing, life's precious gifts all were in front of him, innumerable, invaluable, yet he was now stopping at nothing, he has loved life, all were coming back to him. It was for her he was leaving all.

He had attended several funerals, he was recollecting these. He had never had chance to think of what next after death, he was conditioned to life. It was all to be over soon.

Life was meeting him kindly, never needed a God, a priest or an afterlife. He went to worship but that was on a reflex, his parents took him, when alone he never gave up that habit because it was just a habit.

Life was so full of meaning activities, people, involvement, relationships ,difficulties, solution to be found, never ever a thought for the afterlife.

Still in this moment it was such, nothing to repeat of his life, no after life for him he supposed. Death was to be the end of him.

He was enjoying ,why give it up, for once he thought yet it was for her, all world had shattered he would have to die, there was no point living.

Life was abundant in its bounties to him was he not madly in love with the trees with the mountains, the sea, the wilds, even the deserts. He loved the cities. He had travelled as much as his age would permit he loved people, the world, the culture, the customers, the places, the differences, the diversities yet he was punctuating his life for her.

It was an immense wealth of knowledge he had accumulated, he wanted to write a diary some day of his experiences of his view on the world of his attitude to life of what he expected of life. Time has punctuated that with her death.

He was simply to follow her. From all directions his part was racing towards him, everything major and minor happenings were all now caving to him, he was still, but his mind received all from the past, they were simply crowding to this point of time all of them were fighting to push each other. So his mind could focus on any aspect of life.

They were all vividly coming to him, he was nurturing them all with some delight, a sort of good bye, to all those cherished and unfortunate moments both.

He was not ruined or saddened that this will all end, his destiny was to end it all this night. The recollection were merely to rejoice that past, bid them a proper farewell, there was no awaiting the future for him the future had ended with her, he was simply to follow her where she went.

No account of his accounted wealth, knowledge, wisdom, acquaintainces, family would stop him from such a permit, to him this was to end tonight.

He has done his contribution to the world, his recollection could be said a part of his tribute to the world.

With the good he has seen in life, it was but a necessity to at least thank each one of them by remembering them this night, he would pass away leaving nothing but his remembrance to everything, some might notice it, some might not.

He was never questioning his intentions of ending his life, it was simply to happen, it was to be ended, all the reveries were simply to kill time till that appointed hour where he would be no more.

Time passed away with his recollections, now they were little unreal, he saw mama pleading not to do this she was explaining to him what he was going to miss. What life has to offer in future, she consoled him in ways more than one she explained other relationship might make her forget what has happened.

Mama was almost in tears. Daddy pleaded that he would not let this happen, daddy was crying when he said he wanted more and more gifts over the years.

He found himself in tears he knew not what to do, could he pick up the phone and at least talk to them, no it would probably treble their suffering, it would immensely increase their grief.

He was not going to be persuaded. Why has life cheated her, he was extremely fond of her, together talking holding hands would be the world to her, it was an immeasursable pleasure he received in her company.

If she was cheated out of her life, he would invite death, he was not bothered of other people suffering, he would simply have to leave all this beautiful dream like life he had, no one could persuade him.

Love shows strangeness, takes strongest forms in minds, he was torn with grief, he was unable to understand if what mama said was right. To anyone else mama was right but to him even mama at this moment was wrong. She had no right to black mail him thus and avoid his passage from this life. He had to go. Mama is wrong.

Time was chasing towards the appointed him.

No he was not in any fear, what was there to fear, for his life was all, he was conditioned such, he had never thought of what next.

The pain, yes it would be felt but for few minutes at the most unlike the pain this few hours had given him.

Probably mercy killing himself, he thought, he was not happy now, why should he live, he was to end all the pains which life has bought on to him.

He was not in any other feeling, no range of emotions his past, his interactions were all crowding to him. He was not alone. He was crowded by millions of images from the past. Some were trying to stop him.

After all life with all its beauty tends to attract the living. Life in general tries to pull towards itself all that all living, the thought of death, death itself is shunned to the farthest.

Death is signifying an end, no one wants to end life. All living love life. To him his sudden pain brought by the exit of that girl was simply compelling him to end.

He was surrounded by plenty who would had made this feat an impossible task had he just picked up the phone.

He would be rendered impotent in this venture had be but only leave the house and talk to one of his friends. He knew if he went out this plan of his world not only he indefinitely delayed but was hundred percent same it would never take place. In this house a corpse would not be found if only he went out now.

He knew others would snatch away death from his midst, he knew everyone had the power to remove him from this sudden spell which was now on him, he knew that all would fight to make him live.

Death could be cheated.

Death could be cheated.

No, this was the reason that all the more he entered this sphere of recollections all alone, with the kitchen knife shining in front of him.

He thought that before this while this agent of death could never be imagined by him but as any other harmless object in the house.

He was now prepared.

He went on breathing hurriedly as if to dispel any further signs of returning to him.

He was not prepared to change his plans at any recollecting thoughts.

He was helplessly aiming towards death.

Time was passing at its pace.

Now, her, why was he so fond of her, he had no answer one of those happenings in life which just compels a person to like someone.

There was just a brotherly affection a friendly affection, why this extreme step.

He was unable to answer this question. Afraid, he thought these questions were just a confusion carried by the love of life so that his end might not come.

He quickly convinced himself of his immeasurable love for this person, he personified all his affections to her and even talked to those personifications. He was attached to her not for a day or two but over the years.

His unsaid love to her, it has not been confused to anyone else but himself that he valued her most in the world.

Why would he.

Most people have friends, one whose affection is placed at the highest pedestal of relationship.

Most family have some people who value some relation more than anything else in the world.

With him it was just the same he had valued her highly, placed atop, all the world in his mind. There was no reason to confess this to anyone even mama, surely it was a natural thing.

But ending life was it natural.

Somehow the human mind works is always, a question mark, where lies the border line of sanity, no one can ever clear up.

It was similar for our man he was just recalling things till the appointed hour came.

He was tired very tired of all the things which he had till now discussed in his mind.

His "conscience" was clear on this act, yet he would be leaving a lot of suffering and grief for others. Yet this was for him, for her he had to end it.

He was not ashamed of cheating his vast number of people. He was not ashamed his contribution to the society would end now.

Pleasure, he was pleasure seeker, loved almost everything life had to offer.

His activities were varied.   He was involved in vast number of fun seeking, pleasurable activities.

Who does not love pleasure.

But like all things he valued in life they would have to cease screaming now, he had after all till date enjoyed everything, to date he has loved all the world had offered.

He needed nothing more.

He had seen them all.

Regrets, who will not regret losing it all if placed in similar circumstances, he was well placed had a number of years ahead of him to enjoy, do what you want, it was regrettable indeed, but to him was it not obvious, it was obvious that regret was a natural emotion to emerge.

It was all calculated in this way for him, he recollected, regretted yet he had to die, end his life.

Life is beautiful, why deny it.

But to him it had been shattered to millions of pieces, why life full of emptiness without her and he justified and waited for the appointed time.

He wanted to get up and bid his last farewell to all the inanimate objects of the house, touch them, but again he restrained, the mental image were sufficient.

If he were to touch all recollections physically he justified himself it would probably take years before he would be in position to end his life.

It was slowly coming back, his accident in university, nearly put him in hospital for weeks, he had seen something like death before.

Why was he not dead then, why meet her, why go through all this trouble of making a relationship. Why bother pouring affections on her and why life would give all bounties like this to snatch it away without a good reason.

If life could cheat.

This time he would cheat life.

Life deserved to be taught a lesson. He was a lover of life a pleasure seeker, never a brooding person.

If life could destroy him.

He would end it all for himself, in an act of vengeance would destroy this big cheat.

He was now troubled, little disturbed and picked up the knife.

He bared himself, and felt his body all over, he was sure it would be very painful, he was never able to suffer pains.

This knife almost for bidding it lay in front of him.

He picked up the knife, he was now a little fearless, he was aiming at the right position, somehow these knowledge of the most vulnerable point, no one is ever taught, it is just as if part of learning experience, the experience of growing, this knowledge to grows in your mind.

He was pointing it in the most vulnerable point where there would never be a return to life, he was now thinking of her only, in his mind no other recollections, but her, he was annoyed at her end all the energy in the world which would come to a man, all frenzy all extensive powers came to him, unlike what he had imagined in no time and surprisingly he did not feel the pain, he could only see the hilt.

He knew in some moments he would be no more.

Power had come to give him immense courage he was not in his sense to feel the cut, no he did not scream or shout.

He was just thinking of her, he was feeling weaker and weaker, he lay where he was, vision was barely seeing anything.

HIS END WAS NEARING HIM.

Time had raced and the sun would soon rise, he just thought of her.

The whole night he had not uttered anything but sat still recollecting in that place.

Who knows what happened just before the thread of life which exists was about to snap. He faintly mumbled with no one near him to listen "I don't want to die".

A university is born

He was twenty, observant enough to have experience of an eighty year old.

He was graduating in commerce.

Figures came easily to him.

Not much of a poet or thinker.

Yet , when he passed the crowd that day there was something that would change his life.

He saw a placard "aid for the famine" and the crowd had already inundated the counter with piles of money. He was told the truth, it was an enormous sum.

He was thinking of channelling the wealth of public in a more constructive manner.

This was just a seed for thought.

It was going to take a lot of effort though.

A picture was unclearly forming in his mind.

His sector of the metropolis had a primary, secondary schools, a few diploma colleges, but no university.

A catchment so large needed a university.

Small coins makes a billion.

He was popular.

Very popular.

People would listen to his plea.

If rightly made.

He was now to plead.

He invited many known and some unknown people, the idea was stimulating.

A very colossal project.

People wanted to contribute in small manner, they knew it would be good enough to make a small school.

University. No.

It was a project better left to government, tycoons, philanthropist who had unimaginable amount of wealth.

He knew this would happen.

It was like shown a mountain and given pebbles to make it.

He would have to explain power of pebbles to the boulders.

No, it was not easy.

Not even a single person was convinced.

"All right , but I want tacit support." He took a petition with innumerable signatures.

This would be sufficient.

With the petition he was outside the doors of those plenty bureaucrats who abound the corridors of power.

He was to fight a machinery that was inert to the extreme.

Yet, miraculously in a month he had the suburban two hundred hectares at his disposal.

A trust was formed.

Now, the pebbles knew the boulder is not far from formation.

He was at it now.

Somehow his translation of grandeur to minutest commonness was instrumental in making everyone understand.

He would not stop.

Well one day he said these two hundred hectares would have five hundred departments, but he was to start with fifty.

He loved saying, let's have anatomy department now, the neuro anatomy department and osteo anatomy can come later.

It was the fundamentals of his planning that he knew would make the university.

He was smart enough to show a hundred years finished product of the university, he explained how over the decades it would grow and take the final shape.

It was unimaginable, how he would proceed, yet he would.

Step by step the dream would be fulfilled.

The same logic that applied to the department development applied to the construction, granite flooring could be had later, a basic floor was needed first.

It had started, the work was progressing.

Innumerable donors came his way. Well, lots of departments could be made.

He was not doing this to see the finished product in his lifetime.

He was simply a seed.

It would probably take a century to achieve the scale he was imagining.

Now the work was to be planned, executed by professionals, professionals who would now find the donors.

He relinquished his chair.

This chairman retired at twenty one.

 He knew now his dream would now turn a reality.

That was all that mattered.

Chairmanship was intoxicating but what the heck , was there not a need for a large tertiary hospital, perhaps after a break he would start pleading all over again from the new "chair".

Sunderbans

Yet again a mangled body was found.

The tigers have done it again.

The people have named all the remaining tigers in this area, it is the same, last weeks culprit.

The forest officers were badly beaten again. It was not their fault.

Someone had to be beaten, naturally the forest officers ought to control the movement of the tigers.

Ditches fences, electricity, gun, they had all at their disposal.

Life was precious.

The forest officers needed all the punishment they could get.

Who was the victim?

This large mob of two thousand did not know.

Anyone who has reached this place will know a crisscross of water body lamentably leaves irregularly land placed all over.

Tides regulate the land mass in this delta of the Ganges.

Season regulates the land area.

It is almost in these uncertain land masses villages numbering thousands are strewn across.

Tigers are prized, they are protected. At the cost of human lives.

Who was the victim?

He was the local legislators son. No wonder the crowd of two thousand in an hour, as the day programmes it would be a good twenty thousand at least forest officers, government officers, buses, public places have had it.

It would be ransacked.

Burned.

Soon half the government would be here.

He was a powerful pearl in the necklace of government body.

He was probably the third name in the party.

The tiger had chosen the wrong person.

Few good and lots of trash guest houses hotels always had few foreigners, and lots from the city who come for this great spectacle of nature the sunderbans and the great beast lamentably getting towards extinction.

There was a panic.

Guests have started learning this place. The legislator was too like a tiger. Amongst the villages one could almost find one murder he had committed. Rather his hoodlums.

Why only that, it was well known the local police at times escorted to his enemies strong hold and at the expense of police jeep, government gun and the government cartridge a murder would take place.

Regrettably in this hour of tigers menace the legislators killings were forgiven, pardoned, he was a victim.

Helpless at the hands of the sunderban Tigers.

This maneater who had mangled his son was truly innocent in a sense the number of "crimes" he committed was far far less than the number that was attached to the legislator.

Yet he was full of vengeance, he had nearly uprooted the government in an hour.

Chief Minister would be here soon.

Why

Transfer orders to the incompetent officials.

Probably a lot of funds would reach their for peoples safety.

Admitted much needed for ages yet this time the tigers have had it.

The forest officers have had it. A week passed public menace hue and cry subsided.

Of course the legislator was a human being for the years he would feel the sudden, severe, undoubtedly priceless .

Time passed another mangled body was discovered.

For three days it could not be identified whose body it was. Then with much awaiting from one of the villages a frail old man in tatters verified it was indeed his son.

Poverty to the extreme was shown in his face.

It was shocking to see his poverty had drained his range of emotion as well.

He was least concerned of death of his seventh son.

Who was he.

A patch of land, a very small one at that was his.

Uncertain paddy.

Large family.

They went to the interior for some forest produce.

This time the son has had it.

No the forest officers were not beaten up. They had a sign of relief.

It was indeed a miracle, this person loss has been noticed by the family.

Extreme poverty cannot be shamed in words it can only be experienced.

Uncountable lost people were usually attributed to the maneaters menace.

Unaccountable very many that is

It is indeed a thought provoking statement one never known how in this day and age so many could go unaccounted.

Days passed another mangled body, the terror of the nearby village was the victim. He was a professional.

What he could not organise.

Bank robbery.

Election rigging.

Murder.

It was his profession, the surprise was immense, he had himself shot two tigers earlier.

It was a joke that he could be without clothes in the both but must be holding the revolver in his hand.

He never walked without revolver, large knife and a "Double barrelled rifle"

Indeed a feat performer this maneater.

People were more astounded, than in grief at his death.

Few days passed and conversation would be that indeed a fearless maneater that had courage to maul him.

It was later people sighed a relief at his absence .no one was grieving for him.it is said his father was happy rejoicing that nature punished him for killing his own brother.

Whatever the maneater was, news again.

In sunderbans people live with tigers yet they are news only when someone is discovered dead.

Months passed.

Three bodies beyond recognition were found.

After a yeomen effort their identity was established.

All were from the city.

None a resident of this area.

People rounded the forest officers,a lot of hullabullo.

A lot of destruction ensued.

Then what came as a shock the maneater was not the culprit.

They were mutilated by civilized human beings.

Motive would years to get established,if at all.

It was indeed shameful to give a bad name to the tigers.

The tigers were innocent.

You could hear them roar almost in an effort saying 'why blame us all the time' or perhaps the tigers meant 'shameful someone else had done this deed for us'

A lot of effort by the government is made not to let the tigers go hungry.

It has always been that way,they resorted to human beings in their last effort to save themselves from pangs of hunger.

The victims of maneaters are easily identified, quite early.

But with these mutilations it was nearly impossible to say the motive and identify the culprits.

Yes you can say it was hunger.

Hunger for power, hunger for revenge, hunger for money,all these conjectures could easily be gathered.

The maneaters rejoiced at the new development.

Months passed.

Another mutilated body, definitely the maneater.

Victim, a professor, he was studying the habitat and wanted to study scientifically the behaviour of the tigers.

Apparently he was seen on friendly terms with them.

The forest officers saw him within few metres of the tigers.

Something went wrong,the chemistry got mixed up.

His psychological calculation were upset in a fatal turn,the tigers were not to react this way ,anyway the answers were with the late professor now.

People complained at this alien loss, somehow he was at fault. The tigers were an uncivilized, uneducated lot, yet... yet he with all his education reached there.

Why blame the innocent tigers, there is so much unsolved psychological enquiry of the human mind that has not been explored.

A rather futile exercise going up to the wilderness to get an answer from the uncivilized beast.

They have claimed no civilization.

Yet the most worthy species of the planet instead of searching its beastiality reaches to the animals.

People, mostly ignorant village folks, laughed at this suicide, what else, suicide it was.

A great many academician gathered in the small inn and the farewell had an air of educated farewell, lots of people went up to the podium to give a very nice picture of the late professor.

It was a loss to the scientific community.

Months rolled by.

This was the tourist season, national, state and international travellers.

To get a close view much money was paid.

It was happy time for the vehicle owners, hoteliers ,forest officers.

Everyone was happy.

No, the vehicle were not conforming to the safety laws.

People took their chances.

What else.

Three mutilated fatally, three badly scarred survivors.

Again a hue and cry.

It was news.

International tourists were prized, they bought in revenue.

It was splendid place to see the tigers, but not splendid to end life this way.

Talks and talks.

The ignorant village folk stood by ,gathered in large numbers.

One mumbled,'I stay here for necessity and these stupid people come here paying a kings cheque.'

One was surprised'what do people find in seeing a tiger in such a way,zoo is always safer,if not that should be the only way to see the maaneater.'

The ignorant villagers lamented at the suicide.

They forgot for a time being their revenue.

True quite a lot survived on the tourists revenue.

It was immense confusion.

Old memories came up,all the tiger tales were again narrated.

Government was immensely troubled.

Somehow legally all life are equal,but in reality a tourist life is somewhat sacred, international tourist ,that was truly almost godlike.

Government would be answerable, diplomacy would have a busy time, bureaucracy burdened with the paper work would have more of it

Furthermore the forest officers job would be burdened with new safety laws.

Of course all could never be implemented, yet there would be lot of legal aspects.

The immediate uproar was too great. This tragedy would have impact like none so far.

Yet like all things in life this too would settle soon.

Till a new calamity befell.

Calamity befell indeed in a months time, this time some ignorant, stupid, not conversant with the law of the land had shot a tiger.

Who was he.

Not even the best of poachers could achieve such a feat with so many laws and hurdles.

Sometimes it was true a tiger could not be accounted, yet it was not this way a shot tiger had been found.

A lunatic perhaps.

Hunting in this fashion was outdated, not even the chief minister could do it.

Indeed the miracle was performed by a tourist who had used his licenced gun, later described by him, the sight was too good, he could not restrain himself from the game. He was willing to compensate a lot for this joy.

It took months before he was released from police custody after a careful thought on his mental state.

The occasional poaching in this area it seemed was to be in further trouble. Too much vigilance now.

A relief for the tigers.

They get government protection and government respect.

Over the years sunderbans had witnessed a lot of tiger killings, killing of tigers yet one can always think of some laws which we have not formulated for ourselves, the beasts don't make laws, happily they are content by laws we make for them.

Pillars of faith

A very famous temple of the Hindu faith where I had recently gone to "see". The guide book had made it a "must see".

For a person who hardly follows an established religion it is very difficult to understand the complexity of the Hindu faith. Almost you can say hundred of religion in one.

So, I was there at the "must see" as an addition to the album of places of interest visited.

Yes it was made beautifully, the carvings, the decor, the colour all were a visual feast.

This was a pantheon temple, each small chamber allotted to a God. They were all present in their throne, all almost endless number, I suppose the ones absent, one either not fashionable any more or the lesser Gods.

I was in my way of thinking, lots of photographs to be taken, endless number, it was too good to resist.

Turning towards gods I was amazed at the beautiful sculpted figures resplendent with jewellery and finest attires.

It was indeed amazing sight my mind was wondering at this fame it has achieved, the number of tourists with cameras was amazing.

Somehow the eyes miss what the mind does not see. The faithful till now were on my blind spot. My guide was explaining with much pleasure all the myriads god's achievement their exploits. Amazing.

A young woman with a child was going towards the sanctum sanctorum, I was annoyed, my view was being hampered.

It would be a good snapshot, she had to move, yet I saw her prostrating, weeping, wailing before the god, she held the child to the god and was without bother of others present, was seeking blessing for child's good health.

It made me realise my folly. For the next hour I revisited the shrines all the gods were with the faithful.   I saw the faithful, their devotion, their belief, their faith, was yet unknown to me.

My only act of faith here was to remove my slippers outside.

I vowed never will I visit a place of worship with an eye to photograph.

Places of worship from that day are left out from my "must see" places of interest.

The Hermit

It was the usual bustle of customers, close friends, politicians, leading leaders of industry that came up to "the tycoon", he was into computers/Telecommunication/ mining/Airlines. Yes he was not the richest man in the world, he was ranked in first hundred.

His 68th floor chairman office was one continuous space of luxury, bejeweled paperweight to multimillion dollars paintings each item in the spacious clutter had an immerse value all collected over the years with greatest effort and an eye to perfection.

The penthouse of top was just used between 6 and 8 in evening to entertain the top brass of the society.

His house was the rolling 400 meter house 18 km from the city centre set amidst splendid park, the parterre was reputed to be worlds largest.

He had turned sixty five, feeling almost forty, he had always taken great care of his body.

Years had rolled with him at the helm of the corporation he was improving. He could not afford errors, his errors were indeed big money.

He had a slow feeling of tiredness meeting all these people.

He was taking his day off, unbelievable supposed the whole lot, everyone thought something major was to take place, his absence from office was virtually never,the secretaries were with him everywhere he went.

He was apart from this and a flamboyant lifestyle, a serious reader. For the last ten years he was thinking of a retirement plan, somehow he was toying with the idea of renouncing the world to roaming the world as a hermit.

The corporation would go to his children, the house to them and along with that all the wealth.

He was seriously considering the life of a eastern hermit, who live on what nature provides or that received by begging.

He was 65 even if he lived till 100, 35 years looked quite a lot. He just reminded himself for an appendectomy he had 10 years back he was air lifted in his private chopper from his luxury yacht to the best hospital one could possibly find.

He knew what it meant ahead, a life without all you had known incognito roaming the world, the countries he would roam probably at some time the nation's leader had either received him with courtesy or he had entertained them in his numerous ,chateau, chalets, villas, mansion spread globally.

He was till now connected globally wherever he walked had instant access to everything which the need might be.

He knew the implication of the vocation he was to choose.

That night he donned the garb, a loin sheet to cover the lower half and another to cover the top, he went to the garden and slept on the grasses under a tree for food he just had milk and bread.

When he got up he was decided, he knew what was to be done. In a week all legal problems were sorted unanimously, his eldest son was elected the chairman and all problems were sorted.

No it was not announced, he was not a nobody, he was the headlines. That had to be avoided. Well he was headlines even now with the decisions and everything he was doing. If his plans were to be leaked it would mean further explosive headlines.

What was to be done, he was "first phase of his plan, everything has worked smoothly of come amidst lot of publicity and questions. Yet by the end of week everything was set.

Second phase was disastrously difficult, he could see the headlines "Tycoon Vanishes", there was no excuse which he could provide, if he said he was quietly residing in his private island villa – people would flock there.

His children could not be confided either- insanity they would think. Yes they would finally allow him his way it was very difficult to explain.

Could it be in phases, first to the island villa and then reduce visitors to the most inner most circle and then depart his way.

But impatience had set in already.

Eager to start a new life.

It became more and more improbable at this stage.

Finally he thought what he did not want, he made his intentions public.

Newspaper, televisions covered nothing but this for days. He was debated.

Now he was ready, with leave of his family amidst their disgust he did what was needed. He was on the path with his loin garb and not a sign of any money, he was out to the new world.

For weeks he was intercepted by reporters, he knew he was getting full coverage still.

But this died down soon and he was out in the new world.

Now he was truly incognito, unknown, living the way he wanted it to be.

He was soon in the foothills, he enjoyed the view, the weather, he was donated some woolen's by the villagers, he went on preparing in an uncharted course.

No one knew him yet he always had his meals from some one or the other.

His looks even in that tatters bore a mark of respect. The simpleton country side people treated him with reverence and he was always honored.

He never looked back to his part, it was all over, there was no longing for anything.

His life has been exemplary and he prided it as such. Ever since on his journey he had forgotten that pride as well.

Almost everyday, flocks of people would gather around him wherever he went, he had talked to leaders of the nations, leaders of the industry, his own staff and many more, now it was his turn to condescend to the lowest of low and he was quite charming, he guided them in their smallest of work and used his managerial skills to improve their quality of life.

Education imparted by him in hours were what one would not receive in a three years of university training. He was unwell at times, but he maintained his journey, somehow where he got the strength was unknown to him.

Nights were spent in the wild or more often than not was forced by the country people to be their guest for the night, he would be pleaded everywhere to spend more time with them.

He took a step further and went to the desolate wilderness, there were no inhabitation to talk of. He had by experience to learn the edible from inedible that nature provided.

He spent ten years in wilderness, he was eighty now, what was he trying to prove, nothing, it was just what he wanted to do, everything would be the same.

He was hoping no transcendental knowledge, he got none.

He was back in the foothills where he was before, some recognized him, he was again revered and received well with everyone.

Having spent time in wilderness, made him more calm, he was still teaching the people he met.

He knew it very well when his end comes these strangers would perform his last rite and he was not bothered.

All that mattered was he was journeying into an hitherto unknown world to him, there was no past here and there was nothing waiting the future, the present was all that counted.

The defence mechanism

He was twenty five, not very old to have amassed experience of years which bestows on a man a maturity, bestows on a man a beauty, bestows on a man a sense of accomplishment.

He was twenty five.

About to start life with a newness, he was ambitious, he knew one day he would be someone.

He had graduated, was now on a new job, not quite new, three years old, quite enjoyable, sense of accomplishment started to build on him.

Then all of a sudden he met with an accident.it simply took away his power of his right hand.

It was sudden.

Fateful.

Changed his life.

He knew he was not a success story any more.

No matter what he did it was impossible to be the same.

Very very impossible.

What could he do.

He could never start a life anew.

He was a cripple.

It was debated at great length for what he could do, there seemed no way out.

He was lost.

He was defeated.

From nowhere, that unconscious we speak of, that unknown we never ever believe in.

That god which never appears to a "normal" human being, that god of whom we think not once in a lifetime.

He resorted to "god".

He resorted to religion.

He had a large joint family, he had a large circle of friends.

They suggested him alternatives, "start a departmental store with our capital", "start a business with our capital", "start a school with our money".

He was inundated with offers, yet he was not changed.

He wanted to resort to the "free" god, there was no capital needed, neither a hindrance at being a handicapped.

No fantastic service to be performed, simply turn to god and worship him.

His family always stood there to feed him.

His family were always there to help him with whatever he needed.

His friends would see that he did not die hungry. Somehow, food always comes to everyone, whatever they do, it is almost free for the askance.

He turned to god.

He turned to religion.

He was a worshipper.

Incessant compulsion to escape from the real world, praying, remembering god in all his greatness.

Night and day.

Nights were sleepless, chanting names of god in all combination, days would be but a continuous form of worship. Only to eat would be broken from the reverie of god.it was not voluntary at first, later involuntary, almost ceaseless devotion.

He was not unknowingly believing one day "union" with the most high would happen, he believed one day god would favour him some divine blessings.one day he would achieve something extraordinary, the power limited to the prophets, his life was biblical.

He was unaware of outside world.

His family and friends knew he was in severe depression, he was turning inwards excessively.it was futile to explain to him. his world had crashed on him.

He knew he would unite with god one day. God had to forgive him for all past sins. God had to take him into his embrace and bestow upon him some unknown grandeurs.

He was anticipating the miraculous, how he did not know, months turned into years, he had started believing in himself as a some sort of saint, he saw in his actions quite stupidly though that he was divine, he would interpret everything in his own ridiculous parameter, there would be no escape, once in this mess he would conjecture all his actions were ordained by god.

He thought god was acting through him, it was enending. it continued.

Sometimes he was the chosen one, sometimes a messiah, he was nearing god everyday he imagined.

He was taken to the psychiatrist, but to no avail, his preoccupation was increasing day by day, he knew of only this solace.

His wants were restricted to food, provided by family.

He lived.

Yet, only with god.

No one called him a saint but himself, it is now years anyone has heard of him, neither is he in a mental asylum, nor a saint or a prophet, save all by himself.

The last I heard of him was that his younger brother had allotted him a sum annually for maintainence. His brother knew of the considerably reduced wants.

He is still deeply engrossed day and night in his meditation.

Who knows where he will end, mental asylum or god will reveal himself to this self chosen one.

Who knows.

The immortal man

Circa-3000b.c

He was condemned to die, no one had ever escaped these, if one ever managed to escape almost always he would be caught and suffer the torture, the like of which could never be imagined. He somehow knew he would survive, he knew it was his destiny to live, he loved life as no living person loved, everyone knew death as a fact of life, to him it was not such. Others prided in afterlife, he prided in life. The miracle happened he escaped, not only the cheater of death escaped he reached the most beautiful secluded place of the world. No mortal had ever set foot on that place, it was not known to anyone neither to him it existed, he drank from the stream of life, the place vanished.

It had given him immortality, he would live as long as human race continued, he would be the spectator of the wide arena around him, he would be there forever to witness all the happpenings and changes going around.

And he knew he would live and love life forever but would never be able to disclose immortality

2000A.D

In the towns numerous guest houses, one was particularly unnoticeable, someone entered and asked for a room, advance payment was made for a month, his belongings were two large baggages.

He was a handsome, very polite, charming person to talk too. He was shown to his room.

He was alone soon.

He was unpacking and the baggages contained nothing extraordinary.

This was to be a year long vacation in this part of the country.

He was working these five years, a manager at the bank, the work satisfied him immensely.

He was thinking of roaming the town this evening with nothing to do but enjoy.

Having made himself comfortable and home he departed the guest house to the outside.

It was a pleasant evening, he stopped by at the local cafeteria, refreshing himself he was out again.

It was indeed very difficult for him not to be noticed by the prettier sex, he was desirable, handsome and this caused him irksome trouble whenever he went on vacation or worked.

His reluctance was often placed by fairer sex as his loyalty to someone he loves. But they persisted , yet he was always charmingly refusing.

With bold stride he was out again, in these beautiful resort towns one is hardly ever bothered by anyone, everyone thinks the other wants privacy or busy with himself.

Suited him perfectly well.

There was nothing to conceal, like a law abiding person everything was in order.

He was back late at night in his room, his love for life was still afresh , he was not tired.

He would never look back to the past, they were all so fulfilling, he would never think of the future it would be better seen.

His present, this night was just a reverie for the day, it was enjoyable.

He would love a month's stay here.

He was soon asleep, knew the new morning would bring him a further glorious day.

Life is to be lived, enjoyed, he did nothing but that.

After his vacation he was giving a serious thought of joining the university for a course on architecture or perhaps a few year as a farmer will do him good.

Well there was still a year to think about it.

The Library

He was nobody, no one apart from his wife, his three children, his parents had heard his name, he was forty. He had shifted from his home village and was now in the neighboring private metropolitan city.

He had his family in the village, his poverty prevented him from either reaching there or writing them letters which prove expensive to his meagre budget.

His village he often dreamed of reaching there, just to see the burial place of his grandparents, just to smell the sweetness of the morning air, just to meet his long last relations.

That was not to be his wife was an illiterate housewife his three children all young but where already employed in one of the many odd jobs that bound a metropolis of a developing nation.

Who was he, he was a garbage collector, quite shocking but that is still a profession in some countries. He prided from the rest he was collecting from offices, schools residences and not from the garbage thrown out in "dumps" of developing countries metropolitan city.

Somehow there developing countries have a funny notion of urbanization, it started with colonization and primate focus thence established , remained the urban rules of government, industry, services etc.

There is no doubt a policy of urbanizing the rest but it is far too slow to be perceptible in recent memory.

It was our garbage collector, who was a nobody every morning his day world start at seven and end at nine at night, the same monotony, the same routine.

He would start his day going to the cities financial hub in all these great offices, used stationary, periodicals books would be thrown, he with his large sack would start the day.

Some day the sack would never fill on others the sack would fill easily and there would be four or five changes.

He has always been a nobody, no one bothered if the person who collected was trash or him.

He was illiterate he always picked these sack full of loads and sold it to one of the numerous collectors who in turn sold their heap to the industry.

It was this chain which kept him going it was quite a happy life for him, he always had some amount with him.

He was not a very ambitious person, his meals, some dresses for family some savings that was all he needed. His needs were indeed pitifully too less to be mentioned.

He would go to the schools, he knew when it would be the right time for cleaning session in the schools, he would always find his sack full there as well.

On weekends he had different circuit, he was in the neighboring residences. Some sold their waste to him, some simply gave it away to him, some were anxious for his arrival so the disposal trash would not spoil the beauty of their drawing room.

He was illiterate, he noticed his buyer, sorting books, periodicals, into separate piles.

To him all were the same, yes sometimes the gloss of the binding would appeal to his eye and he would think it to be valuable, often he was wrong.

So frankly he never bothered to ever do sorting himself he left sorting to the buyer, he was content with what he received, he was simply seeing them valued in terms of kilogram load of the sack.

He prided he had given his three children proper employment, no the education and the rest which is taken or granted by others never ever occurred in his innocent mind.

They would all fend for themselves was he not of that age when he started and at forty was he not content with his meals and his savings for the bad days if they were to come.

His dream would be of seeing his desolate village, a village it was but of around three thousand people, he had a small house there. In time he had sold his plot o land when he shifted but had retained his house in the village.

A house if one may call it such two rooms timbered ceiling with stones slabs coming it to protect from elements of nature.

The walls surprisingly were "pucca" a small house, but not many in the village had the wealth of this kind of house which our "nobody" had.

He wanted to see it year after year, but it was never possible for some reason or the other. He never desired to sell it, one never knows when these cities might simply collapse on itself or for any unknown reason to him he might have to leave the city to reach his place of birth.

Occasionally he would meet someone from his village who would use his little dwelling in the slums in the manner of "guest house", he would entertain them kindly and listen to all the recent gossips of the village.

This village surprisingly had indeed "prospered" a few shops, police outpost, a village bank.

He was always interested with the smallest details of his village, how far the roads have widened how many new roads were laid, whose house has recently turned "pucca" and so on and so forth.

With every passing year he would love to hear that some vehicular facility made it possible for day to day transport.

He would very minutely scrutinize that the village headman has plan for a rice mill in the village.

He would sometimes hear that the trains stopped in the nearest town daily instead of earlier twice weekly.

You could say his pastime of examining his village to the minutest detail continued every day, probably no block officer of the district would have a similar knowledge which he seemed to possess with every passing year.

Yet he had never been there. He longed to see it but that was all. His wife was never concerned of his or her village she had you could call urbanized completely, an occasional movie and the tiniest television which money could buy had made her a complete city woman.

The children in a year or two had plans of having their own dwelling in the slums, somehow these vast private cities are a contrast, some people with life's saving find it impossible to buy a house where as the other half with pitiless some finds a "house" for itself and surprisingly quite content with such an accommodation.

His life was a very satisfied one, one only had to look at his face to know that he had seen nothing but happiness one could almost envy his happiness.

He prided in himself that his children were also independent, satisfied, happy.

One can wonder how with all the metropolitan offered for a price, kept our "nobody" away, no one ever questioned him, to him it all existed with almost the similar alienation as what would be earth to someone from other worlds.

He was uncaring, he himself had not seen a movie for almost twenty years, at most he would take his wife and children to the zoo.

That was his world, not that he knew not they existed, he knew they all came with a price, perhaps over the years he had resolved to such a phase that he knew even dreaming of such things would he almost impossibility for him.

He was happy as he was. Why bother of the starred hotels his princely room has entertained so many from his village in some time or the other over the years, his home was guesthouse to them. Not many rich people could ever dream of entertaining so many in their place with all the wealth they possessed.

He was never proud of that either, to him sparing his meal to his guest and allowing them some shelter was nothing but quite a common day to day work of life.

In this simplicity he passed forty years, he rarely ever thought of anything else.

One day he had a child from his village with parents as guest, he was quite amused from his sack the child of thirteen was eagerly sorting just like his buyer.

He watched intently.

The child had piled almost three books, few magazines on one side.

He wondered what was going on.

He questioned the boy, was surprised that he could read, he was literate, some how he had missed from elders of the village there was a school which has recently opened in the village.

He asked the child if those trash were any good, he was surprised to know their price if one actually brought it, he was surprised to know they were readable.

He had during the days work been to the neighboring library in the rounds today.

He knew what a library was.

He gifted the child with whatever was liked by him. When his latest round of guest had departed he said to himself, will that he knew he collected some which are valuable, yet he had never understood it all in this fashion.

As if from nowhere this nobody had a plan, almost crazy if he said it to others, but he had a plan in his mind.

Everyday now he would think of materializing that plan, it sounded so simple, yet he was not sure.

He was initially reluctant, but he tried all the same.

He went for his usual days work and then devoted an hour to his plans, he went to the neighboring houses and surprising rightly said what was needed to be said, he said I have a small house in the village, I want to make it into a village library madam you have children in the house, if you think some books or anything which could be kept there you posses, I would like to have the same.

In a moment he was helped by what he needed. Now there was no looking back.

In amidst the same query, his answer was what he needed, no one was offended.

With passing days he had unknowingly collected what a small library for children would have.

For once he reached his village, turned that "pucca" house into library, to be cared by the villagers.

He often heard children rejoiced there but his pocket never permitted him to go there again.

A nation grows

He was an enterprising youth, fortune favours the brave he had some capital by virtue of inheritence. He was twenty four, he had a vision.

A diploma in computer science, makes you no professional in a big way, neither confers management skills, nor trains you for a huge enterprise.

Somehow the success stories are those very untrained, who have a vision and apply the experience of life, summating it with wisdom of others. He was one such.

He was a businessman with a difference, he wanted to procreate like an almighty God a difference to the society, he knew his profits would suffer a few percent less but he knew it would be in the long run very satisfying.

He was impressed a nation according to Plato was a population of ten thousand, it had immense meaning, it meant to him self sufficiency for that number of population. A nation to him was summation of times that figure.

Everyone would be productive, what is urbanisation and what is development. Nothing but man's varied activity increases.

If you see the same thing from the centre to the roots, it is difficult, the numbers in a field is imperceptibly small.

By multiplication of work in smaller units creates adequate jobs.

He was always laughing at the failure of highly modernised units with less and less number of jobs claiming efficiency. Yes that is the ultimate goal, but not when number of jobs needed is immense.

It was his vision, his plans that multifarious activities and labour intensive units that would be nations answer to development.

A nation who for thousands of years has not made popular the pulleys for the well, or wheel barrow for load. To him was extremely inert to process of development.

Centuries of static behaviour had made people least involved to activities.

Development was an active population involved in nation building.

Times were changing, but the vast majority was still ignorant.

He wanted to do this part, he knew he cannot change others, he knew alone it was to be limited.

Yet he started all the same.

Intentionally he chose the remotest, least developed of all the places.

It was a village of thousand with smaller villages contributing to total strength of around ten thousand.

When he reached, there were no roads to connect it with nearby town, there was no electricity, no common water supply, the houses were all made of bricks and thatch, the catchment field forestry was about thirty square kilometre of virgin forest, fields, it was nature left to itself.

Nearly all were into farming, three shops were all in the name of mans varied economic activities.

He purchased as much land available in the area, it was cheap, very cheap by national standards, he started on his vision.

A factory for bricks, a factory for granite floorings, a garment factory, was to be the pilot projects.

He had acquired quarrying rights in the region, a small quarry would suffice for the years to come.

He knew if without training, he could manage on enterprise with some difficulty, he knew his agrarians labourers would with some difficulty learn the new jobs at hand.

Sure enough, within the initial gestation period, when the things were to be completed, his workers at the granite factory, knew cutting and polishing, his garment factory boasted of excellent tailors.

Seeing his enthusiasm, government stepped in roads to nearest town and the extension connecting with state capital was complete.

He electrified the whole village, people do pay for adequate service.

A chinaware factory, a pin mill, a rice mill, came next. It was religiously seen all employed were from that ten thousand people only.

The jobs in few years were hovering at two thousand, the 50% of the entire productive manpower was under his industrial net.

A national bank opened its branch there. He made, primary, secondary school, a college for higher education, there were largely by assistance of other corporate giants and government.

He made sure a diploma college for training in skills was founded too as an appendage to the college of arts, science and commerce.

With time a lot of shops grew, expectation of people rose, with increased spending capacity. He himself financed and helped people of the village to form their trading house.

Now it was amongst the best towns of the country. At forty he was not stopped at that.

Ambitiously, he opened a railway connection to the district, head quarters and the state capital.

An airstrip, connecting the state capital was immensely successful.

Every year as if gifting himself on his birthday a new project for the town was chalked out.

Parks, zoo, small museum, theatre, cinema halls. He had surprisingly noted his return for capital had been extremely satisfying, he had not lost in fact he had gained manifold.

I went to meet him regarding some problems I faced, at seventy he was remarkably young he solved my problem with his acumen and was showing a model of building, he was very happy once this club was made, he could play golf here instead of flying to the state capital.

I generously thanked him, wished him luck and left in the chartered seater he had generously allotted me for my flight back to the state capital.

At take off it was not surprising to see his interest an housing society has done wonders, rows of small beautiful houses in splendid park setting were a visual treat.

Roots

He was at the pinnacle of success in his field, well not exactly it is a handful who reach the summit, he was where you could say he was comfortable, he was not wanting.

Not wanting in financial security, not wanting in worldly needs. He had them all quite comfortably.

There are very few who look back.

Looking back is not fashionable.

Looking back at humble beginning quite crumbles the very pillar of success. That pillar to be sustained admirable needs to be nourished by a falsified ego.

He was forty leading limelight of the city, quite content, had all at his disposal.

His beginnings were like other self made person, very humble to the point of starting life from penury.

He came from a village, even a village it was not just few clusters of crumbling baked earth walls with nothing more than a thatch to prevent elements of nature invading the shelter, by any definition this house was functional to the extreme, this shelter had a baked clay oven in one corner and few beddings, a small trunk fot the savings amassed in decades of existence in much penury.

Surprisingly it was a time when ninety percent of the population lived in the rural areas and everyone was just a little better than the other.

Existence mattered as in survival, the land to be tilled, ploughed,harvested and the rest to receive what nature in this semitamed way would give. A little cattle rearing for meat and milk would suffice the rest.

Trading was not touching this secluded would people were content with what they had.

The wants were few, trade was minimal. Somehow even in these archaic time textiles were already to invade the corner of the land.

In this lifestyle was his was his father living. He was sent to school, honestly everyone could send to primary and even secondary education. Yet most dropped out for all sorts of reasons beginning from real penury to the fantastic.

Just talk to set of people of that time and question why it was not considered to be educated, quite fashionably. Some would say it was alien, not needed, out of place, and so forth.

Yet this man did the primary, even at this tender age his eagerness and performance beyond expectations, splurged on him a free ticket to all his childhood needs.

Considering his background this was nothing less but a jackpot. No one in the field wants to spare a pair of working hands, but compensated by scholarship stipend he was not stopped, rather encouraged all the way.

His mother was instrumental, illiterate herself but she knew "District Collector, lawyer". There two things were the only thing she knew apart from, shopkeeper, the teacher.

Somehow even the remotest secondary school in the world, statistically has nearly good chance of sending its pupil to the highest level.

It is almost a universal phenomenon all people have fixed ideas of rising has to be from premium city institution, just look around and it is true that any secondary institution has similar chance of sending its pupil to the top.

He was to be one of them. His performance here, paved an easy path for graduation. Again all free.

In this stage like others he had odd jobs together with studies, a practice honestly more consolidates a persons personality rather than destroy or dilute the education quality emparted.

A backward district teaming with nearly a million population, here he was first to do something which no one had done before. He was to be chartered accountant. First in the district.

Once trained, he opted for security rather than garbling with uneven private practice.

He chose the banks, he had reached the uppermost ladder and now he was two steps from being the chairman.

Age was on his side, he would retire at least the second to chairman if unlucky, with little luck he would be chairman.

Methodically he has risen and knew every step would take him to that first.

His children wee all educated properly and he made sure they received the best.

He was now 4 steps below that target of chairman children now grown up would all wish him to be the same one day.

Fate, what else, that was not to be. He had to make a choice of coming down from there retire and be with his family to protect their pride, to help them from crumbling.

A person so methodical reached methodically, knew he would be chairman one day, now stood at the same rung as others helping his family not crumble down.

Why him.

He was the lion, he was the only one who could hold the fragments. None other had the talent, nor courage, nor the practical mind he had.

No he had no choice, it had to be his sacrifice. Moreso sacrifice of his children who yearned to see their father as chairman one day.

Very boldly he left the "chair" for the roots, those very roots that will fashion his family that will enable his children to reach great heights.

Sometimes I wonder if I were him would I do such a sacrifice.

Strangers

It was a cold day, the chill was perceptible, work was a boredom today, he was chief executive in a large firm.

What he needed was a nice drink to make himself comfortable. He headed for the "favourite."

He had occasionally strayed into habit of drinking alone, he loved drinking in company.

He was there sitting comfortably, quite happy the adjoining seats were empty.

He loved it, he hated, hated strangers sitting nearby all inebriated, striking a conversation.

That irked him and put him off his pleasurable reverie if he drank alone.

It was the last thing he needed, distractions, sometimes his most fantastic deals to be planned ,were meticulously planned here ,with him having his "large".

This was not to be, someone sat beside him and he hated it immensely.

No, it was nothing personal, anyone else would had made him feel the same.

It was uncomfortable to him.

Surprise.

The stranger was none other than the famous news reporter, known to almost half the news world.

Yet, unknown to him.

He sat there and was more disturbed that he was not alone, he had someone else sitting beside him.

He hated it.

It was his habit of being alone, strangers they often don't know the art of solitary drinking.

Meanwhile to the reporter it was an extension of routine work, it was time to plan his work, the stories received needed a lot of chasing to all the right places, once you reached you feel silly that you have not thought of all the angles.

A good piece of reporting is a work of art with careful farsight, to be able to do what, when and where.

He was happy to note the other was more engrossed into himself, scribbling something on a piece of paper.

The executive was today lazing his time, it was a good feeling, relaxed, he was not planning anything.

He was scribbling, he tore what he had written and then in another piece of large sheet he printed in large blocks his wife name, shading the paper here and there.

The reporter was relaxing too, he was rejoicing at the success of his last assignment.

He saw the name and his drink almost splattered from his mouth, he blurted out the printed name.

The executive knew it was too good to be true, this stranger was just like others, could not help intruding and start silly conversation.

He stood up to go away.

"I am sorry, please sit, it is simply that I know that name, if it is the same person who I think it is"

He in turn printed her phone number.

The executive embarrassed at the coincidence, said to avoid any further embarrassment.

"She is my wife."

"She is my cousin."

He was silent and then he said "oh, we are not strangers then, never saw or heard of you though."

He explained newsreporting was not entirely a static job as the other had. It seemed his acquaintance was already known to the reporter.

Well, what else did he know.

He knew a lot it seemed, telephone had done wonders in sharing his privacy with the stranger.

Now they sat smiling, genuinely happy to have made each others acquaintance.

It was good it seems that they met, lot of common interests.

Each mentally complimented the other for the charismatic personality.

It was meeting of two giants.

Each in his realm a giant.

Good they had met.

They asked each other if they were free for the entire evening.

It seemed both were and the conversation was then to be endless.

The most important was their varied experiences, sharing them, gave immense joy.

"Generally I hate reporters."

"Why."

"Oh, its only for something that happened in the past."

"Well. Could you explain."

"Oh, it's nothing serious, it happened years ago. I had risen to the middle rank and there was this industrial espionage, if hushed the matter would had not affected my position, yet ,there was this nosy, good for nothing, gave it to the press, ten years ago, july, still can't forget that episode."

The news reporter scribbled the name of the firm, figures and some names.

He almost got the shock of his life.

Yes, it could not be true, unless, yes, what else would it mean.

"True, it was me, I can't forget either, that was what shot me to the middle rank.

The other started laughing, there was nothing else he could do.

Well they both settled and started thinking of forgiving each other.

That was the only way out.

Then came sharing of personal experiences.

It was quaint how over these couple of hours they had reached this state of friendliness.

It is a small world.

They were discussing invitations, probably holidaying together.

Both were married.

Then from discussing children, erupted discussions on their own childhood.

The reporter said it is a miracle that he has shot to where he is today, he was a small town boy, named the town.

The executive hearing this choked and felt faint.

There was only one school in that small town.

Yes they both went to the same school.

Both burst out laughing, the name had struck earlier but that was impossible.

In school they were best of pals, till as quite often happens never met after their school life.

What could be said.

They hugged each other pleasurably.

Both yelled, not bothered of others in the bar "strangers indeed".

The Alien

He was thirty, an accomplished person, successful in every way, he was heading on his road to success.

It was a vacation of some period that changed his life forever.

He had a cluster of families living around him. They had all adored him all this while. They were everything to him.

Yet when he returned it was not the same.

His distant cousins were pretentious to him, he was trying hard to be the same yet he was pretentious, no amount of his put up mask would conceal his mockery, which he did with the children, his expressions raped him, he was the hypocrite, it was not coming spontaneously, he was being intruded ,his feelings, stark-it stood all ashamed.

His uncle who would dote him, now would not even recognize his existence, his adoration towards others were not being reciprocated. Somehow both the parties felt a little ashamed of each other, because the truth-the bond of love now lay absolutely nude, it was hypocrisy or not, neither party knew.

What could be done.

His own brother were was eyeing from a distance the seclusion, the solitude, yet was never willing to intrude upon him, why, because they knew they were now living together with no bonds whatsoever at all between them.

They had been close, too close all their life. They would both be pondering over some stupid speculations and be involved in it most of their time.

They both had ample time.

The urge had died down for either parties. It was simply a matter of unsaid, unfamiliarity. They now knew none existed for the other.

His own father would avoid any conversation, it was never to be the same again, he was almost in a complete void in his father's presence. They were both in complete knowledge this relationship has been destroyed forever.

His own mother was a silent spectator of the solitude, she was also mute to everything. She knew he had lost her and she had lost him.

Aunt and uncles knew it was all lost forever, they were never to be the same again.

He was alone, forever.

They would all be the there for each other but not for him anymore.

He was dead to them.

They would soon be dead to him.

What was this that is so inexplicable, he was with his own people, but dead to everyone, he was a total stranger to these people.

Why it happened, it cannot be explained, was it the vacation that killed him to these people?

Was it the extreme fondness he had for them that died in him.

Was it their love that unwantingly killed him in their memories.

It cannot be ever deciphered.

Yet he knew now he was alone in the whole world, dead to all who knew him.

He lived and would live only to die one day.

An act of faith

Many a times I have gone to Darjeeling, many a times I have promised myself more trips, no it is not with everyone, yes once, twice or thrice would satisfy all their desires of a foothills holidays.

There is something I guess within me which gets attracted to that place, I like all the hills vying to get attention, I like all the curves opening up a new horizon, each twist unfurls a myriad change, unimaginable in plains.

To me it is almost a pilgrimage going from Siliguri to Darjeeling, Siliguri town is just where the foothills imperceptibly merge with the plains.

Once I leave siliguri I think I am not sure the distance of some 70 km to Darjeeling is not one continuous but a series of km halt, I make it a point to drive just one km at a stretch and then I lazily enjoy the place. The ride at most directly takes 3 hours to make, yet I have never reached there before 2 days.

I am not a botanist, I would be at a loss to name all these ferns, trees, shrubs that is seen almost everywhere, I just lazily feast my eyes, somehow with all this population outburst this eco damage, the landslides, the mass destruction of forestry to tea gardens, has never lessened the appeal, yet all the scattered towns do have an air of decadence, yet the complete picture has not yet lost its grace.

You have to have time to just see the unfinished views, they are simply too appealing for description.

I never wanted to reach there as soon as possible, yes the queen remains the town of Darjeeling, with all its shanties, mayhem of shops and extreme cluster of unappealing row of houses, yet the queen is Darjeeling.

On way to this place I have to halt for the night, for others it is never so, my purpose in it is the innumerable curves with majestic view that pulls me to it.

I have always wanted to make a sort of record by delaying this trail to the longest possible, once I made it in four days.

I feel extremely saddened others don't exactly share my view, else there would be some sort of smaller development along this trail.

Be as it may, it is my eccentricity, I was now on my, I have lost count of what number it is, I was back.

Comfortably in the same cottage, I am in Darjeeling more home than home, it is always the same cottage, it is little further from the proper haunts of the place, you have to walk a km to reach the mall.

Here I was resting my tired mind to the lovely views.

The Himalayan trees have an air of their own, as I confessed I am no botanist, I simply could not name any yet I am in love with their height, the shapes, the leaves, the trunk, everything about them has a unique quality that cannot be described.

Solitary if they stand they almost look like the presiding king of slopes, if they are clustered they appear to be some giants walking up the slope. Their beauty and your imagination could see them in almost any form you desire.

Then there is this small animals and birds with all talk of their being destroyed it is not always the case you do see the local lot almost everywhere.

The fog is best seen than talked almost, how the different consistency of fog changes the landscape dramatically is almost as if canvas upon canvas of same image in different hues have been made.

It is even so resting to the tired mind that the weather for most part of the year is pleasant.

Everything about that place left to nature is perfect.

Of course where would the population outburst go but densely abound in the same place. I never blame this manmade phenomenon too much, beauty or no beauty, survival comes first and the rest is secondary.

I have to see tea gardens almost destroying the natural forestry but instead of deploring I see the beauty of the tea garden instead.

There is something about the hills for others it might be otherwise, I cannot reconcile to anything but the monastic religion that widely prevails there.

Little sanctuaries of faith they abound the hills. A certain peculiar custom of theirs the "hymns" written on the narrow flags, always blowing with the slightest wind, it is their belief, with every blowing wind the hymn is chanted, be as it may it is very soothing to find such a widely prevalent practice, this too is almost merging with natural beauty of the place.

Anyone who has entered these sanctuaries of faith cannot miss the rolling drum, overall the monks peacefully sit in these places and chant to the lord with blissful scriptural reading almost non stop.

I have more often than not delighted myself with visit to these monastries they almost call upon your soul to the spirituality.

It is most amazing with people of nearly all faith in this place, for me it is but one which I see as the true faith of this place. Not many would agree with me and frankly I might be wrongly harrased if I were to support my point of view publicity.

Seeing a painting or picture of the grand monastery of Tibet one can also visualize you are looking out of the window and getting its glimse. It is almost invariably present in every other house.

And the almost universal Tibetan teapot, quite an admirable piece if you ever came to own owe.

It is the place to get hold of good Tibetan literature, the "thankas – the paintings and lots and lots of exotic pieces of works and pleasure.

Almost any hill shop is a veritable museum.

Ghoom at the higher altitude has the largest monastery of the region, a vestibule with on one end a drum and its opens onto the inner sancture with a wide assembly and, somehow ever the little details of carved pillars, painted wall, ornate ceiling all lend a exotic picture.

Sitting behind is the Buddha large, looming well above double your height, severe in its facial expression, he simply agrees on blessing one and all. An anointed forehead all give this Buddha a very spiritual look, he is calm not bothered of the assembly that hurries in paying respect and back. He presides with an almost exemplary calm, benedicting both the devotees and the tourist who flashes his camera on him. He is inside the sanctuary yet his presence is felt in the entire region, chanting, flags and so on.

Nearly all the monks live in not altogether medieval dwelling but built on lines of the modern dwellings counter part.

Somehow my spirituality begins to fade, it simply turns a little shallow unless I see exotic architecture, colourful walls, medieval dwellings, stone buildings.

Here it is halved, somehow I reconcile by making my own images.

I also like the monks in their garb all to one look to sit somewhere and start a chanting.

It was on this particular visit, I went to the monastery, I prefer the time when it is less crowded, it makes me easier to receive what the Buddha wants to give.

I went inside the ornate facade gate, stepped down to the courtyard, taking off my slippers I entered the vestibule, and the revolving the drum, I entered the assembly hall.

I was looking up the ceiling, the floor, the walls admiring it all, surprisingly just one person was there at that moment no monks either.

I am not the type who has hallucinations or not the type who easily gets into error of visual reception.

From the eyes of Buddha rolled blood.

I was alarmed, I had never heard of such a thing all my life, never seen it ever earlier.

I was trying to reconcile myself to this miracle.

My fellow who stood beside saw it too and surprising he said "look the foreheads paste has melted down" saying this he left the place.

I was there alone for some while and I too returned.

It is now fifty years since I have not yet grasped who was right.

The blue blood

He was fifty four, four children, satisfactory inching towards retirement, a very happy life was left behind him.

Myriad images of his life's experience all hovering between good and fantastic, a very favourable time indeed had elapsed.no regrets neither of self or family.

Then the unexpected happened.

It was as if this dream like utopian state could only be a myth, it had all shattered one day. That was the only reality.

From a well placed position, it was down to the lowest of the low. Not even survival was possible.

How? Fate. Destiny. What else things got a little jumbled, the position slided, coffers emptied in an attempt to salvage home and necessities, comfort vanished for bare essentials. Bare essentials turned to meagre to maintain dignity and self respect.

That is how life is unpredictably unpredictable,happiness marred.

He was left with the name.

A name not like others, a royal line running in his ancestry, he was from the erstwhile ruling family, last royals before the republican state was established.

Till now his name was not used in any way for the little comforts he had achieved. Yes quite tacitly the post of vice president of the company owed a lot to his title. Yet in the modern world this was given to him in quite a hushed,

concealed manner, not hurting his ego.

Well that was before the crash.

Having airs of his lineage consciously and sub consciously, over the years he was still reconciling to his condescended position of vice presidency. He was always little uncomfortable with the setback that modern world had brought in his life with the collapse of monarchy.

Now in almost a pitiable state which could be visibly felt by others, his own state could be well understood.

Funny when he was well off, his condescension was apparent, yet he did not realize what the title he held, held for him.

Now almost in a penury the self respect and dignity which all of us would give priority to restore. To him his title gave him utmost courage, an inner respect,not known to others, almost unknown to others.

He had it, from where, no one knows.

He did what he thought was best.

Childrens were sent to relations, who would give them his share of affections too.

He knew his wife will not be able to do, what he could, he sent her to her relatives. She did not complain or oppose, she never had.

He was all alone.

He had to be alone.

There was no way out.

Life was not intending to be miserable, had he sacrificed his dignity. There were scores of people who would refurbish him, what was lost, was not the vice presidency a subtle refurbishment of lost dignity.

But not in this state.

It meant direct help, all hands offering to him, all doing charity to him. This time it cannot be concealed, it could never be hidden.

It will have to be nude, stark, naked and candid charity.

How could" he "ever accept this.

There was no thought of acceptance in his mind.

Others stood by him, trying to offer in all capacities, only to be refused.

People adored him for his name, his personality and now desperate to save him from his plight.

It was an impossible situation, he could not be even approached for the same.

Around him he had built a shield, an impeneterable shield that was impossible to enter.

His frugality increased, bare survival became impossible.

It was a miracle he was alive.

He was to drag his body weight onwards, to exist.

Now he was in a state where he had to physically conceal himself from others.

It is quite a feat of nature how time changes, the closest to you leave you first, and others follow suit when months change to years.

He was now a nobody, now his name had ceased to exist in any conversation whatsoever.

Time continued.

He was inching slowly to death.

Crumbling.

He was now nothing, except him name which would simply be dead with him.

The Bride

He was twenty two, handsome, smart, just finished college he was a very calm headed, good temperment person.

Presently looking for that first job, somehow the thrill of the first job is immense, that very thought of getting the first paycheck is undoubtedly the most thrilling experience you can ever have. All on your own. The world at your command your freedom from an unsaid bridge.

That very thought of working and experiencing the real world is immense.

He had a lot of friends, now some in far of cities, few still in the same, the intention of meeting had deteriorated to few as all were occupied and were forming a secondary ring of friends.

Quiet beautiful the entire world seemed, he was no longer thinking of what would happen, it was all how it would all happen.

He had known quite a few girls his age in college was not the steady type.

Yes he was not the flirtitious type, very commanding in command of his life at all times, in all aspects.

He was not sexually involved yet with anyone he was not ashamed of that, rather proud to have used his discretion.

The job that elusive first job was his, he was very happy, his parents were country folks he was alone in the big city. His job was his new circle of friends. The usual routine of life continued some pleasure, some work and some monotonous boredom. He was content.

It was late November, the chill set in and was quite a view it was, sun setting, gentle wind but an occasional chill, all perfect for a very romantic session.

His thoughts were not with him he was just walking towards the cities redlight, it was quite unconsciously he walked towards that part of the city.

No, he was never there before, somehow he was walking towards this new unexplained region of his metropolis, why was not a botheration, he was as if on an impulse walking that way.

In few minutes he was not only there but found himself sitting besides a young woman in a shady, shabby but a livable small room, if you can call it a room. A small window opening only just another window, the panes and the curtain drawn, seen his window was to be curtained as well.

A small bed, a chair was all this place contained.

There was a short pause after entering the room seating themselves by the bed when she said "First time".

He was bewildered, surely that was not possible to know from the face, walking few meters together all in acquaintance of less than one minute, he was greatly surprised was unable to restrain him felt very uneasy, awkward. He finally summarized it was not a coincidence, she must be a veteran, a master at deciphering that facial expressions. His annoyance turned into appreciation of her skills and could not help but guffawed "yes".

Time flew what was spoken was but a few mumble and he found himself unhooking her at her neck level.

Suddenly as if almost an impulse he found himself hooking the her dress back again.

She was surprised, first time for her, it was her time to laugh almost twice the time of his laughter it lasted.

God, she was beautiful with her laughter he thought. When her laughter subsided he asked her without pause "How much if I came every night for a month, and we just talk, no, no you calculate your charges and I am willing to pay".

She was in this profession for almost three years, some naughty, some very naughty, some loathsome, some she gently appreciated herself and some were of devoid of any emotions worth describing.

She was dependent on this source of income, she was not ashamed she was doing this it was almost as if it was a job of receptionist in the hotel or in an offce.

She was in this for money, that was all that mattered she had no second thought when she had started this.

Tonite was different she agreed and said the same "we will leave the calculations till the end of the month I trust you, you can be here all night for a month".

"I am not sure why you want to, you said to talk I am not sure about myself what I will talk yet I like, come if you may , it does not bother to me, every night yes, for a month yes, do come, so what do I say now".

"I want to mostly know your experiences". She was laughing, her laughter could be heard in the whole floor one would imagine, it was very loud. It had a ring of amusement.

"I suggest the deal is off I can suggest you some magazines, some videos and some books" she laughed.

You are one of these looney philosopher, the poet type you will be wasting your money here".

"No, no that is not what I meant, I meant to just talk of you in not the same way as you say, yes the same thing, no I mean your business but not that".

Now she controlled her laughter she knew she was embarrassing him she said "All night you win, for a month every night".

He heard a sign of relief as if a great transaction pending has formalized so easily, he was elated and his face did not deny any of his feelings, he find his hands rubbing with a boyish charm.

"Are you a professional or part time or whatever you might be, she nodded at having understood is first enquiry admitted to her this was just a profession and since he was paying for the conversation she made elaborate statement to that effect that she was under no compulsion when she started it, there was no other choice for her she had thought at that time and she was quite professional and she had never once regretted being one and she also said matter of factly, three years she has took count of her customers, she was on the contrary quite happy now has her spending power and has not felt the urge to leave this now and told him she has a substantial savings and in the most of natural ageing process she would be quite comfortably left with what she was making, she had invested wisely her savings. It took her some minutes when she was finished she thought it her duty to service this client with all the answers was he not paying for it.

For some time they were both silent, it was because she waited for his next question, he was severely confused what to ask next since this new teacher of his has quite a knack for summarizing twenty questions to one answer. It was a long wait he turned and scrutinized the room, he stared at the ceiling, he intently gazed at her dress for a long time noticing the colour, print, design, as if not satisfied he was studying her hands, her face and was now quite content.

"I am twenty two I work in one of the cities largest trading firm, quite a good post, I draw a substantial salary, I am very interested in astronomy, I love music, I am without modesty a good violinist, I would like to have a home of my own very soon".

Now she was bewildered, it was her turn to answer the questions and not listen to what this new "boy friend" of her was doing, it was little difficult for her to think what was happening.

"Do you ever want to give up this profession". Mentally this girl was anticipating this question she was surprised that the question came so soon she anticipated this question would be at the end of the month, just before the farewell morning"

"No I am quite happy, no she stammered how could to anyone like this goody goody guy would she she happy. "No I am quite at ease with what I am doing, it does not bother me, on the contrary if I went back in time, were to start life again I would be doing this".

He was assured, she for the whole time was under a shade of pitying this girl, he wanted supposedly to comfort her, give her an assuring hand on the shoulder.

She on the other was not at all comprehending this fellow feeling, it was impossible for her to think so because she was simply not in that frame of mind, never was she not happy saying happy this time to herself all this while.

He found his hand reaching hers he held it gently but with confidence and in almost a mumble found himself uttering "suppose if you were to give this up for any reason"

"I cant answer that, there is something which should happen if I am to answer, without something happening it is impossible to conjecture"

Well now he was losing his 'pitying her' slowly but steadily he left her hands stretched out his legs and hands lifted crossed behind the head.

"Have you ever enjoyed, I mean that your service" "Yes sometimes, very much" she was silent again she somehow knew for this particular man this was a wrong answer, it was difficult for her to lie and difficult for her to say what she said, she was not sure if this deal she had made with him was a good idea or not, a whole month, possibly for few hours she could answer pretending what would be appropriate for this man, not to offend him but a whole month, she first got up and in an impulse barred the window, drew the curtains, she lit up the bed side lamp and put off the after lights, this dim light was very relieving to her, she then slid towards him, held his hands for a few moment she then moved a little further towards him and embracing him gently kissed him.

"No, wait" he uttered, he pushed her away and again sat with his feets stretched and in a show of defiance put his hands on to his waist. That was it she needed to be taught he said for mistaking him for her other clients.

This time he made sure the chair was as much away from the bed as the physical space in that room would allow, he was defying her natural instincts.

It was to be a subtle war between the two with proper explanation of the purpose and the deal has been made with all intricacies explained it was necessary to let her conditioned reflex lesson be taught, lesson to take a pause, a retirement from what she was doing.

"Were you in love with anyone, I mean the urge to see him again and again"

"No" this time payment or no payment she would not elaborate on this answer he deserves this she thought, he should understand what I am. He should understand the difference between this world and the world where he came from. Could he not understand that he should be grateful that because of an impulsive "yes" on her side this man was sitting here and the ridiculous deal of a month was made. Did he not understand not many would ever even agree to this ridiculous proposal.

She was thinking fast, very fast how to answer him and make him understand she would be making him comfortable in this place for a month.

Now it was her turn to be a little bossy with him so she could herself find at ease with him, after all this would not be one night stay with someone. She was finding ways of entertaining him, help him pass his time.

Yes she thought why not divert him for some time to playing cards, she look at the pack it was frayed she had played alive for long hours of some lovely nights. He agreed and for two long hours they played quietly, an occasional laugh, some joy, at the end he threw the cards in his hands away, gathered the nest and quipped " if I can't be like others, that is too bad, I am me bad still, I must try to do what this place is meant for, what you are meant for, I am forgetting the deal. I do what you are waiting for, I am all for what you stand for, you are professional prostitute, you are to give me pleasure, I cannot think otherwise all right, so should it be.

He rose confortable from his chair, the love of his clothes, standing start naked infront of her in few minutes, his manliness showed no signs of inability,he was standing there capable, beautiful he looked his whole body quivered, and shook at the sight of the beautiful, desirable her, he was at it ,not like the first timer, he tore her top dress, literally tore it off, not concerned if this assault would mean criminal offence to her, he was frenzied animal tearing her clothes off, not few minutes passed she stood there in his naked beutly, yes she was beautiful, still with all she had lost of over the years, she was all he wanted this moment of time.

She was still, he caressed her whenever his hands could be, he was all over him, he drew her by the bed was atop her, she was atop him, he was fondling, trying to posses her in all ways. The very storm begins in him, had just started, he held her tightly as she lay beneath, in all his manliness, he was maddened by her sight, probably the very pause of her given with all the games, with all the conversation, had risened his desire to newer heights, he was frenzied, not in his senses.

As if from oblivious as if from something not known to her, she separated from him, stood at a distance, grabbing a sheet she covered herself in a way not covered by any dress she threw a sheet on him almost covering from neck to the toe, he was not in his senses, yet she was in all her right thoughts, she simply adjusted her sheet to be covered, in a way never veiled before, the most lovely veil it could be to her womanliness and all she uttered was.

"The deal still stands this was not in the deal". He without any further understanding of statement in almost a slave like manner. Got up, dressed and not in few minutes was sitting in the same chair as if nothing has happened, she was not trying to dress, her sheet covered more then any dress in the world, she sat down and said "it was my fault, I have become used to others, my natural instincts have failed me, I am trying to undo what was undeniable, would you like two drink". "Yes" he said. Two drinks were poured no words exchanged till, almost half an hour had passed. He was sober with all the drinks although he had never drank as much in his life before, he was greatly, relived, no more frenzy, no more desire, the drinks had made him impotent, as if by a spell, he was just a child in front of her, no matter even if she was to provoke him he would not be assured this manliness was no more, he thought if you can call that manliness, he stood limp, impotent to this great tutor, which he had discovered in so end of his educational life, he was wanting her to speak something, he was waiting for her teach some thing new, like an obedient student he waited patiently for her to teach which he knew not.

She started talking loudly incessantly without stop"It was my desire regretably, I will not say it my fault, it was all so unnatural, you sitting and talking, I have never done it before I would like to be myself, I wanted you to forget and enjoy, how I wished I would change your instincts, you are like an alabaster statue waiting for all in your deep self. Don't deny you want it as well. You are pretending you are not here for it, you are just like the others, you are not what you seem, I don't know why you are acting, I don't know why you are pretending". Saying this she was sobbing, loud, than little milder, still sobbing. She could not control herself.

He was for a moment in a trance, not comprehending what was happening, then he was stark again in front of her, he removed her sheet, and they were one, together in a union, he took his discretions for reasons unknown put off the light, it was all darkness, the were entwined in an ever rising passion, it would not subside it would not ebb with any passing morn, it was even rising frenzied, storming till the blissful stillness came with almost an unsaid harmony for both of them. They were now silent still entwined, the lights were put on, they would not separate for almost an hour, no words were exchanged, he was waiting for her to say something she still had the deal in her mind, it was not a question of what was to be said, it was simply a question of what next, for her everything was over, to him probably over as well he was not unlike others there was no deal to be talked off, he had behaved like others they come and go, it was almost animal like there was no question, he felt almost ashamed of being like others deep within his reasons was that he was not like others, there was no point of thinking like others it was useless, all his hours of initial effort have failed he was just like others he was one of them. A customer that is, he almost felt like taking out his wallet and pay her to her good.

Still he composed and was trying to take a halt in his feelings he found himself still not like others, was it not a months deal. In the first day he had failed, she failed him. It was her fault.

For her side, she was not bothered still and probably enjoying the thought it happened, she was very happy, it was not like other she had ever on her years paid or otherwise, it was almost a fine love she had experienced. She had experienced love, pure love, nothing else, there was no animal like sex, it was almost god like. The union was almost unexpected, truest. She would remember this even when she would be ninety, this was a beautiful moment for her. Yes he was sitting there, she had forgotten him, he was probably now relieved and go back sooner than she would imagine, often all that deal would be off, he will not be their but this experience would be with her forever.

He was not to go, he picked up a towel himself and almost as if nothing has happened continued. "You almost reciprocated like the first time" "Yes you can say I was a virgin till now this, was the first time".

He was not talking anymore, silent but flattered he was admitted his act, admiring her flattery and was very very happy all the while. He lit a cigarette and was puffing with a smile a smile in his face never before.

She was also draped and she said, "I hope for once that you were happy, I would really like to know you were happy, you have enjoyed, you really liked"

"Yes to all you have asked". She was extremely happy, her girl like enthusiasm returned, she heaved a sigh and was very happy and again returned to her silence.

He felt that nothing happened and was back to his imaginary deal and continued. Did you ever have anyone who came here and did nothing of that and did something else".

"Yes she said quite a few, those who were unable to do" it and she smiled this time a patronizing smile almost insulting his acumen for asking that.

"I have failed in my purpose I admit but I am here for some other purpose my enquiry".

"Why".

"Why, what"

Why the enquiry"

"No reason, I just want to know"

"And what write a book, write an article in a magazine". "No it is for me and me alone" "Was it your lack of courage to approach me that you started the deal". Was it the first time of you, that you proposed the deal, you must be truthful, may be unconsciously, be truthful".

This time he was confused, she was right he was in the office this afternoon, no prediction of the deal, why was he being so holy of all this, there was no reason, why was he being dishonest.

Honestly he thought to himself and wondered she was right, I am being a hypocrite, I don't know why I am here, why I asked all this neither I am writer of great repute nor a breeding philosopher, why am I being so confused. Yes I am lying.

He stood up and said, "you are right I am lying, I don't know why I made all this act up". He was silent.

She knew his mind as if she was reading it all the while, and she knew what to say – she took his hands gently and made him sit by her and said "you are one of those who have never been here before, never again will you come. It was my fault in corrupting your gesture, I did not allow what you came for, I never knew what would had happened if I had not forced you".

He was not convinced. He would now never be convinced of his intentions. He was not happy that she took the blame on herself. "May I continue with the deal for the month".

"Yes"

"I feel almost ashamed"

"No in a month it could had happened sometime or the other" matter of factly she said lighting up her cigarette.

He like her and almost with an unknown brand of pleasure being with her, he searched himself, first his body, then his pockets and finally took his wallet and in the pouch was a gold coin a memorobilia, he had from a friend, it was aptly depicting a Godess of some sorts, he gave it to her as a token of appreciation.

"A gift from me".

"You are feeling guilty are you not,covering it with all sorts of gimmicks, I will not take this to hide your shame".

"No this is for you, no other feelings in between".

"Thank you". Now she took that with no remorse, no other desires. She was happy. First time she had received this gift or any gift from her "customers'. She wanted to celebrate, she poured herself a drink and to his glass and was without any words enjoying. She was smiling, very happy, she truly was enjoying this moment.

Somehow she wanted him to come every month of the year, the year to never end. She could forget her savings, she could not him be here for full she could simply let him be here all the time, all the time in the world he wanted to be, stop, she said to herself she was dancing , he would stop coming the next day or the day next, it would all end, there would be no more of the deal. She would simply be all by herself with her hundreds of customer for some more time.

He was regained, rejuvenated, he sat up on his chair and was almost smiling, he wanted all his questions to come, he wanted his questions to come to his lips one by one, none would come. Then from nowhere his stream of questions had started, he asked I was always wanting if your lot had a some sort of consensus,unanimity of sorts ,you know meetings ,gatherings,

"No, but I have some close friends who are into this".

"Do you discuss"

"No, would you discuss to your colleague of your work day in and day out".

"No" he kept silent.

Why was he being so stupid, it was just a profession, they were from separate worlds it was just like any other profession, they were not from the same world, it was almost as if he was being obtuse, not trying to think, what she was saying it was ever so simple he said to himself all she was trying to do was her job it was a job, like any other, where was the great fun.

There was no other explanation it was his stupidity. She was being extremely simple. She broke the silence and said "What is it that bothers you, your morality or your religion, or your attitude if you are an atheist"

"No nothing bothered me till I was not with you, it is just when I was with you all confusions arose".

"What is it the thought of playing so much a botherations".

"No it is the thought that the most ancient profession is still existing where is the stability of the society we talk off".

She had never given it a thought, yes she was right, if she wanted there would had been other professions, may be less paid, if all agreed to choose some other professions there would be some left in this profession. He was right. Now till never before she found herself very shameful, she was paid for that, no it was not right, sometime he was right, no one has a right to allow this profession to continue.

It is almost disgusting to think that she was in this profession, very ugly she felt. Yes he was right in all comes, it was fault of others and her that she was in this.

She felt almost ashamed never in life she had felt this feeling for her profession. I should never have been happy here I should had been ashamed of my doing. There are plenty of jobs even begging would be better, it is my fault.

Both ways she felt bad for herself and the society, both were in the fault. The society less to be blamed herself more and more. It was truly her fault, she could had done anything else in the world but this.

No she was not religious, neither of high moral virtue neither was she of the type that was guided by life's higher values.

Yet this person was right, if she was of any inner strength she would not do this.

She felt disgusting.

She sat down and was sobbing he spoke nothing, she was sobbing it was not right she felt, it was one of those moments in life better left alone, he was still quiet, silent, he knew he had convinced her without convincing, the mental battle had been won.

What has he left with, nothing but a lot of tears, has he helped her, no, he has not he has really destroyed her, till now she has continued with this way of life, now she had a guilt to this, this guilt would shatter her this guilt would destroy her.

He was cursing himself of coming and the deal.

He knew not what to do. He saw her silent for the long time and she started lighting cigarette one after the other, soon in the silence there he realized he was in the wrong place, he had injured her, he has disturbed himself for no reason, he was to be blamed for coming here, for starting of that miserable deal.

Soon she composed herself and said almost in the tone she had entered the door with him. This was the "first time" she held his hands and kissed him very slowly, all over, lips, cheeks, and the forehead and held him very tightly.

Her instincts told him she wanted to hold this man very badly, she was not ashamed, she was liking to hold him.

He was also now one of the customers he forgot all of the deal and was handling her very tenderly, he reciprocated all her approach with the similar feelings.

This lasted few minutes, he asked her in a murmur, "will you leave this and be mine".

She simple asked "How soon will you be shifting to your new house".

"Tomorrow"

"I suppose the deal is off"

"Yes I suppose so".

The Gayatri mantra

Idon't know what its meaning is, from my childhood story books of mythology in my possession, a tradition abounds about its miraculous power, memory fails but it is said to have power enough which in modern days would be noting less but fantastic.

I am too lazy to enquire about it any further than I know. Be as it may.

I was holidaying in the hills, it was less crowded that day and from nowhere a chanting of this hymn flowed into my ears.

As a rule I have nothing against the religion of hindus abounding the peninsular India, yet I have neither been attracted or repelled. They are present and I don't bother much about them.

There is too much of traditions, mythology and fantastic, in my most examining eye, even if I subtract the literary jargon, it is too fantastic for my taste.

Yet when this beautiful voice, yes, it was the voice that was beautiful, I have never heard such a voice all my life, the hymn was rendered with repetition of the first line only.

Hundreds of times just the first line, for the first time in my life did I feel much beauty, such pleasure which cannot be expended.

Whether I like other religions or not is not the important point, I appreciate all that could be appreciated.

This song pulled me towards it, I still remember struggling to leave the place before it finished.

The endless repetition continued and I was after a long time away from place.

What was so captivating, good voice, the rhythm or the hymn itself.

I was recounting my memories for its powers attributed to it.

As a student it was my passion to study other religion out of curiosity. My knowledge of the hindu texts and beliefs are probably without much difficulty, must I say vast. In combining, history and the present I could be an authority.

Yet never was that attraction.

This "mantra" made me a little different, not that I did not respect the faith of millions yet I was moved only this particular day.

How a single line can call upon your thoughts to examine and see the entire philosophy in a different light is amazing.

How stubborn beliefs are if they vary with yours, perhaps someday I should go then all the hindu texts with this first line being sung.

I have not tried yet, someday I think I should.

Funeral of Prince Zayd

Centuries ago in the east ruled the king emperor, indeed deserving the title, he was lord of fourth of the world. His son the only one, to assume the title was the most capable of assuring the new role of king emperor.

Skills practical, military, acumen, judicial, administration, legislation, humour, will, charismatic, he was the epitome of monarchy.

A culmination of ages of wisdom had accumulated in him. The king emperor was proud indeed.

A sudden onset of fever, in presence of hundreds of physicians within few hours, prince regent, son of king emperor, was no more, he died.

He lay in his bed chambers surrounded by pavilion, lake, rivulets, fountains, verdure and the many bronze object de art.

The bed chamber colossal, open on all four sides to the porch, which led to a balcony and that opened to the terrace.

The bed royal was enormous delicately carved ivory, mingled with woods and be jewelled gold.

With finest tapestries around he lay on the bed. He was lying with the bed sheet covering him to the chest.

His luxurious hairs fell to the shoulder, a shimmering golden hue it had.

His face had reflection of death a gentle smile lay upon his face, that smile has not left with spirit of life.

All around incense fragrance and the smile filled the room.

The king emperor broke down but recovered,he would grieve after the funeral. Funeral would be as world had never seen, he was unknown to the fact the like of which will never be repeated in future.

He was to rest in royal bed chamber for the night. The whole night was spent to make the most marvellous chamber in palace grounds where the body will lay in state for three days.

The preparation was on war forting tens of thousands were constructing the farewell palace; it was to be ready over night.

The pillars were erected

He lay with a smile

The beams and vault stabs were placed.

He lay with a smile.

The morning around he was to be embalmed, the place where he would be in this earthly abode for three some days was complete.

In an almost unknown manner for three days millions were to see him, his farewell was to be remembered by all.

Grandest farewell possible.

The chief architect was busy laying the path to the final resting place, the mausoleum was to be small yet the most expensive it could be even imagined.

The chief architect and the treasury and the goldsmiths were in a frenzied pace to complete the task. All this happened and the gentle smile on the prince remained as he lay in state, mutely witnessing the homage of millions.

He was to be taken on the final journey. Tens of thousands would lead him there with all pomp and gaiety, elephants, camels, horses, people,all in their finest with all possible show of power possible.

Millions would throng the streets, a carpet of flowers the road will be, A most lavish display of wealth, power strength would be at either side.

As if expressing what as king emperor he would had controlled an almost endless display of treasury, wealth was to greet him on either side of road.

Prince Zayd maintained his smile, was he laughing at the uselessness of such or was he smiling at leaving all this for something in the nether wounds.

The kingdom was at his glance either side full display of military strength perimetered the area. He was not to leave for the heavenly abode without witnessing all which he would had commanded.

The most beautiful girls of the kingdom all were gathered in one corner, death was to witness the beauty as well.

Prince Zayd slowly inched this display.

Finally at the door step of his final resting place.

The holiest of the holy and the most royal were to inter him. The king emperor was by his side.

He stood examining the most beautiful, most expensive resting place, it was flawless.

No he will grieve later.

It was time to let his beloved go to the heavenly abode in grace and dignity.

It was all over, buried he was.

The next morning saw no trace of pomp what stood in the emptiness was the mausoleum.

The king emperor was seen entering, he had given orders not to be disturned, he was alone.

Days passed, he was still inside

Till like all things in life, he came out to start a life without Prince Zayd.

The Musician

The weather had a whiff of chill and the air was calm very quiet, you could almost hear the ruffle of the leaves even if they were pushing away the silence of the wild with punctuation of chirping of birds and the rusting of leaves with an occasional sound of passing animals made it almost a most secluded, unexplained region of the world, almost because from as if miles in one way from nowhere a road stretched and it was in the other end going nowhere.

It was me and me alone going towards the only house in middle of the nowhere land.

I was on my way to see an old friend who was now a valet in the lonely castle in this forasaken place.

It was said near the castle was a tiny village which had all the people living there, they were all employed the lonely master of the house, generations lived in this seclusion. Now with time the master of the house was the cripple, behind him everyone called the same, he had but his two hands with power, remarkably escaping the disease, the rest of the body was said to be deformed in almost an unhuman shape.

His feifdom now reigned over the house with its three staff in all. The nearby village had long perished there was no one now living there. The village of twenty houses were only visible when you utterly scrutinized the thicket that had formed around then

They were very dense, the paths had but became the floor of the roots and ferns and the thornery that had spend over it. It was a sad sight to see some very beautiful houses and cottages all covered all around with thickest of plants over it. They were all vying for the limited village space, the arrogant tress had broken the walls of the houses, they were simply all over.

I had almost covered my journey without knowing how with my slow pace I have done this, I had reached the end of my journey and the road was now at its park, the hump, gave a fabulous view of the whole region.

It was most beautiful, with the sun set all you saw was the shade of grey, all over the gray was dominating the whole view.

My tired feets were now almost giving way, I could now no longer carry on with the journey, I took a halt, I sat by the roadside stones, they were a relief, my fatique quickly collapsed and a rejuvenated me was was born. I was listening quietly to the song of the wild it had its own rhythm. I loved it all the more because it was ages I had left the city.

From nowhere there came a soothing music, the music was almost in a very low decibel, it was somewhat mixed with the music of the forest, it was not annoying that the wilds had encroached on the music it was almost as if the master musician with his instrument was orchestrating the whole wilds into a mega symphony, hitherto unheard of my me or any one in existence, it was a privileged moment for me, in any eventuality I have knowledge of only one person residing here, the cripple, the other members of his establishment were not in the hobby of music which I had gathered from my friend, who was this person on the instrument.

I started walking towards the destination, the music slowly dominated and the music of the wild was fading into a hushed silence. It was true that I was in this region the most celebrated critic, I find no shame in confessing my ear for music is not only known by this region but I suppose in greet many countries, who was this composer, not the piece I would place from my knowledge to any one I knew, I was simply not believing that I had heard this in the first place, amazing to know such music, merit on itself if it was the grand master or contemporary masters yet this was a "composer" oblivious to the would yet there he was placing, what could only be called the grandest piece of composition yet known to mankind. I was at first extremely ashamed of this ignorance, ashamed I was not acquainted with this grand master who could it be.

I was further amazed the music was coming from nowhere else but my destination who could it be.

Now the music was in complete command as I reached my destination, the music of the wilds had ceased to exist if at all the intensity of the sound had almost ruffled the ambient.

I knew not in more than a minute would I meet this person who has unimaginably severely conquered my senses, baffled and at the same time marvelling this new chapter of my life I was in a trance like state when I entered the house, unknowing, not bothered who had opened the door. I was entering the house only to seek who was at the instrument.

I enquired the three member staff if anyone else was invited, their presence obviously cancelled any thoughts I might have of them of their artistic capability. It was a growing suspicion that now rested on the "cripple" I vehemently opposed such a supposition in my mind, I was not willing to accept that my physical senses forbade such a notion, it was amidst a great shock that I came to know from the members of the house that it was indeed the cripple.

I was led upstairs and by the end of corridor I was to discover the genius, he was with the instrument and was in complete command of the same, his physical self did not imaginably permit such a feat, but as it would be indeed it was him, he was playing the instrument with almost his rest of body contorted beyond imagination yet his hands were at it.

Some miracle, something almost divine, I am not such of a faithful, I put it entirely on the limbs taking all the spirit of the body, all essence of him lay in his hands he was simply excellent with his hands if the disease had destroyed the rest of the body.

Seeing me, he dropped and almost in a shock was at the other members of staff with greatest of rebuke possible, he was not kind at all. My applause had given least diversion to this animosity at the moment. He was not to be discussed, he wanted the anonymity. After an hour had passed in rebuke, consolations, reprimanding, comforting in both directions that he calmed down.

"No it is just my secret, I am not known to the world, only these know I exist, that too because I need to support my life, I knew no one except these three.

You I had invited because I knew of your passion for music, I wanted to know what was happening in the world, I convinced you to come in almost a pleading manner, I wanted to be unknown and simply acquaint my self with what music were offered to the world, I am now finished. Promise me if any one can be trusted, I want a solemn promise, I will remain unknown, you know from my condition, I will not live for long I only want anonymity, is it much to ask"

"Indeed what you ask is much I would be cheating the whole world, I would be cheating the present, the future of something like of which the world has never seen.

"I am afraid, I have to beg then just that you may keep your promise"

Seeing him such, I knew I will have to keep the promise, a promise I would be tempted to break at every passing hour and unlike him. If I were to live for long what a torture for myself it would be, to keep that promise, I was not thinking at this moment of giving him my word I was thinking of the life ahead of torture that I would have to face in keeping any promise. But there was no option, he would die peacefully. I will be a ruined man in my death bed .

This "cripple" had no notion what he was asking for, he knew not what he was hiding from the world, any sane person and physically able person would find ways of extorting all from the world, yet this man was giving away all he had to no name.

Once again I begged him, explained to him as if he knew not that his composition were simply too good, priceless, the like of which the world had never seen.

Yet he was unmoved by my plea, I was forced to give my promise.

I requested him to at least let me record for myself, I promised it would be one day destroyed.

It was futile, he was unmoved. I was almost in tears. "I permit you just one thing tomorrow I will render all my composition, I am sure in a few days you will hear them all.

I was looking up to him like a slave, master was giving me a treat of hundred life times.

We parted

The night was like the night never before, the night was as if never to completely pass. Every second looks like eons

I was waiting for the morning. Have I ever done this ever in my life, no never, I was never to be known so impatient, cruelly the night passed at its pace.

I wanted to think of the music I had heard almost I could beat its rhythm with my fingers, my mind had captured it, it felt as if I would die in this blissful state I was all the more sorrowed at the thought I would have to keep the promise. What would a man do, promise like this come only once in a life time. There was no way but to keep this promise.

Night was torturing me again, my agony increased my anxiety increased my sufferings increased I was pained to think it was still hours when the maestro would be at his instrument, and I the audience would represent the present and the future mankind who would be the sole audience to the performance, sole person to applause, sole person to know he existed the compositions existed. I wanted to die now forget the botheration of listening and then keeping such a terrible promise. But it would not to be, I will have to survive and bear the agony all my life. I paced the room in frenzy to tire my physical self so as my mind gets diverted and I would be exhausted and be sleeping for some time.

It was as I had thought sometimes later I was exhausted in mind and body and I slept.

It was morning and I was with him, he was eager to know of what was happening and eager to listen to him. I told him now and then I would summarize it at his interlude and was persistent that I listen to him immediately.

He started and was at it. The magic had began his instrument was the whole world to him, he was at it, the rest of the body bore no resemblance to the human kind which he belonged. The hands with dexterity were at the instrument, the music was there for my ears, this was the miracle, I beheld him with an awe he was not bothered of me, as if I was absent. The compositions which were all his had a most stimulating effect. My mind tired of sorting the unthinkable, disgusting and the chaste, here I was to listen I was spellbound I knew not one but every piece would be a better step to perfection. Here I would be not to think that even one would not be chaste, pure original, fascinating but all would be perfection in itself. I was lost almost in a trance, I was neglecting my entire self to my mind, even never happened before I could feel the music, I could see the music, the music had entered all part of me, I was in raptures

The interlude came and I briefly summarized him to the best of my knowledge, he wanted me to candidly say what part I disliked. I respectfully bent towards him and gave him my world, every part was flawless I was hearing the chaste, pure and have conjured in my imagination what was going on all the time. He titled the piece and gave me an account of what his next piece was about.

He started again and the music was there to see I could see with my eyes what was being depicted, it was an unending succession of blissful raptures on my side, I was in the similar trance like before.

Piece after piece it went on, hour after hour day after day, till as it was to be anticipated it was all about to end, the delight was finite, I know this had ended I cursed myself again for promising him what could possibly never be done.

Like everything in life, time to part ways, time flew I heard later he was no more.

I am still alive but with a very heavy heart I wish I had never known him ever in my life.

The Party

He was a doctor, a doctor never retires, he might relinquish his practice yet he remains a doctor, he may leave his job yet he will be the same.

People will flock to him for treatment and advices.

A happy retired life he was leading, he had a coterie of very good friends, the circle of his friends stood in plenty. But the habit of twelve bosoms was regular in meeting once a month. The date was decided at every visit this has continued for good ten years now.

It was satisfying, very satisfying, notes were exchanged, at other times they could meet too, but this "ritual" of once a month togetherness continued.

Same city, it was not a problem.

Absence had yet not happened, the get together was his idea. No one failed to compliment him every month for the ritualistic meeting,that the doctor had started.

They were of the same age hovering between sixty and seventy, spouses, friends, children were not invited in this gathering.

It was intimate.

They all arrived, it was nine o clock, the party would last for three hours.

Dinner.

Music.

Peaceful.

Conversations were from mundane to fantastic.

The lawyer was today visibly bulging with an idea, he said, he " had a proposal, we are all law abiding citizens and if we all shared something of our darker side, I am not sure if I understand what am I saying"

The twelve were quite keen on his idea.

The lawyer elaborated that they would share which normally one does not share even with the closest friends.

The twelve got perplexed, have they not been sharing till then.

Then they answered themselves with a smile indeed they all had something very private not yet shared.

The doctor stood up and said he was sure the twelve had understood, but was it really necessary that they ought to share darker side, whatever it meant to others.

The others nodded.

Amongst a lot of whispering, the banker stood up and said since we want to share our darker side let it remain forever in that room, forgotten forever when this session ended, never too be remembered by anyone even if that meant a customary, voluntary forgetfulness.

All agreed.

The legislator volunteered to start the confession. They all laughed always a leader.

"Confession, it is I know not what else to call. In a way I am glad, this has happened, I never had the courage, our closeness it might be said is deeper to our spouses, children and rest of mankind."

A cheer of approval, smiles and the doctor almost had a tear of joy when he heard this, it was the truth.

"Well, it was almost forty years now, I lived with my uncle, as you all know, parents died in an accident again which you all know."

He stopped.

They were all silent.

"I was reckless, finding easy way out, I was given a good education, a secure job awaited me, I needed to be rich, I was a dreamer, I knew salaries add but slowly. My uncles wealth was to be the answer. He was not a distrustful person, he was not a person who lied, he told me he was going to donate all his wealth to the local charity, it was his dream. I would have to work three lifetime at my salary to reach what he was giving away. I knew what was to be done. No one had yet known of his intentions, in fact everyone would say to me, one day you will inherit this, splendid, people envied me."

"I had told you earlier I inherited his wealth, I told you he died in an accident"

Everyone looked grief stricken.

He sat down.

He stood up again "Well it was done with utmost planning, it was this way.

The doctor stood up "I think you have said your darker side, it will be quite adequate, you need not elaborate any further, mind you my respect and friendship for you has not changed or diminished.."

The others applauded.

With a visible tear the legislator sat down.

"Must we continue" asked the shopkeeper.

"Yes" said the lawyer "the party continues till all are heard"

Everyone nodded.

The banker wished to end his part of ordeal as soon as possible,he requested his turn.

No one disapproved.

"In my profession there are innumerable occasions where my dark secret could lie. Sadly it is not there, I am honest in my work, I have retired with grace, yet it was the bank."

"I was forty ,you can say little tired with my wife, yet loyal to her, there was this pretty girl who worked under me, somehow I could not restrain my advances to her. In my position for some little favour it is possible to make others do something in return. I used my position to get her my way."

The others smiled.

'Then It was an almost incessant urge, I went on using my favours, my position with others'

This continued for a year till I realized I should stop this'

'Well, it ended'

He sat down drank the the entire glass, in his life's fastest'

The others kept smiling.

The lawyer stood up and said he would like to continue the relay.

The others agreed.

'It is well known to you and others even in my professional capacity I don't go by the book, there are instances which I have shared with you of my professional 'misconduct''

'Yet I would like to share something that prompted me to start this game.'

'I have now it seems be getting ghosts from the past, of late I am having dreams of a eighteen year old girl, when I was eighteen ,I loved her dearly, moreso I wanted her, it was lust more than love.I had tried all gentle ,civilized approach, yet she was not consenting'

'At my age what seemed normal, I resorted to rape, rape it was. She was frightened, I could not explain her excessive fright, it so happened that for years she was not normal again, lost her memory and reacted dramatically to my insult.it is only of late I have dreams of her.'

The others were silent again.

No one knows who said it but a faint 'Why have we started this' was heard amidst the silence.

The doctor was feeling quite unwell and he requested to speak.

No one objected.

'My life was as neat as could be, I was not much of a crafty or charismatically smart person that is why I became a doctor.my professional life was full of compassion to the verge of a very sainted man. Yet it was one of those nights I was returning home, my car sped in the curving road, I was in a hurry, someone was suddenly crossing the road, I could not stop, I ran over him. Unknown to my instincts, unknown to my very character, I left him and speeded home. I saw it in the morning papers, he died, the investigation was futile.'

'The way it happened, I chose to forget, forgotten till this day, what I should had done, I have never debated.'

'I have forgotten so ghosts are also kept aside.'

He sat down.

The others were too surprised, too saddened to say anything.

They knew they will have to forget this as well.

The shopkeeper was next.

'It is not a crime, I must confess. Years have passed I met a you might call a witch doctor, he claimed supernatural powers and quite proud that he did a lot of evil with that'

'He gave me a voodoo doll and said indeed it could be used as such. He departed saying it will work just once. I threw that away in some corner. Years passed when I saw it again I was surprised to see it again.'

'I sat with it and wrote my wifes name on it, I had nothing against her'

'My belief at the supernatural'

I started banging the dolls head on the ground.'

'Next morning I came to know my wife had died at my in laws place of brain haemorrhage'

'I have married again, I don't know if I am to be blamed'

The eleven mumbled 'guilty'

The professor of mathematics was next.

'I wanted the chair badly, it was only by being the head of department-could I get respect. My peer was better and vying for it. I resorted to paid hoodlums, my only rival got a head injury, I got my chair.'

He sat down with a geometric precision.

Everyone was aghast.

How little they knew of each other.

The hotel owner was nervous he pleaded to speak.

Permission was granted.

He said it was thirty years back, he saw a lovely couple in his hotel.

He was charmed by his wife.

Infatuated at her sight.

He did what no one would do, he recorded their sexual experiences, it is still with him he still enjoys watching it, he is not ashamed,has no remorse whatsoever.

The antique dealer said I have already told you of how I have sold the fakes with a genuine stamp.no one doubts me, I am the ultimate in verdict.

'A young man had inherited a fortune, I went to him his house was a veritable small museum, things collected over the ages all lay in all their glory, I devalued and cheated him.

The writer was next. He was not a household name, he received little royalties.it so happened the eleven would on occasions support him financially.

He was the only single in the lot, why, maybe of his insecure finances. No, he at times had plenty, it was the uncertainities at other times.

'It was ten years back, I was very low down, I don't know why, but it was a combination of my solitude, my finances, my failed ambitions and perhaps the unknown.

I decided to end my life, I resorted to poisoning, I took the adequate amount of pills, three days later I woke up to see myself again, weak and tired, I was too surprised and perhaps as it might be an act of god, I chose to not to speak till now'

The others clapped.

It was the doctors turn now.

'Unike the colleague the host of the party I have always taken my profession as the most charming and I think it is a very ambitious man who becomes one.

I am a surgeon, egoist by nature, I have misused my profession in almost any capacity you can think of, it goes unnoticed, yet my dark side is outside the realm of medicine. I love my daughter.

A friend of hers had insulted her,I poisoned that girl. Today she is useless in all respect, and in a state worse than death, she is alive.

I have no regrets ,it was for my daughter.

The only industrialist stood up and said it was when I started, I sold anything from pins, buttons to prostitute, of course it lasted a few months only.

He sat down.

The judge stood up.

'I have an undisclosed accident, I gave guilty verdict to an old enemy though he was innocent, I used my position to rape my juniors, I have amassed a fortune by swindling my rich relations, and I have abetted few criminals to settle few old scores of my own.'

He sat down.

All twelve knew this party was better forgotten

His World

He is two, just got up from his afternoon nap crying, calling mama, daddy is usually not around in this time, mama has to be called feeling terribly hungry, not had a proper feed this morning too, was feeling quite unwell.

Mama usually comes around at this time if screams all day long, she must be awfully busy today, no wait, hears her shouting, oh she must be in a funny mood she usually does not do this all the time.

Mama is finally here, she has come with the bottle, good, she will probably pat him, feed him, no she is in a better mood today.

Well the hunger had subsided, he is feeling immensely better, no point talking to her today, as it is mama takes time to understand him and today she is in a foul mood, it is useless, pointless, talking to her today.

Oh, she is getting ready what is she upto, he is not looking happy either, she is throwing the clothes almost in a disgust, she is all willing to take her out somewhere.

Well, this place gets stuffy at times, now it is almost choking, a breath of fresh air would be good for him today.

It looks like a bright day.

The park would be a good idea, lovely green, carpet of green all overs with bright flowers scattered all over. She would start talking him colours, he would have to identify that was boring, extremely confusing. If there is anything in plenty, it would be counting.

Then there would be sun, the sky. Yes, would like to learn, but not this fast, give him some time, mama was hurried almost giving her entire knowledge to him.

If she knew anything, he had to know that. There would be no escape, she was adamant at times to learn everything.

Daddy was no better, he had to make sure he learned everything to the last. He made sure mama had taught him the whole day.

If he used the hands it would be improper, he had to learn the table manners.

Can't they see it was more fun the way he wanted it.

Games, why can't they bring him what he likes. Mama wanted something of a learning game.

Learning and learning, he was tired. He wanted it at his pace. They had their own pace.

They could never leave him with what he wanted. If they went out, someone had to take care of him, someone always nasty, he wants to be alone, better that way, but no it was someone he did not like.

Fussy, what is so difficult in leaving him alone. There was more fun being alone, doing what you wanted.

Of course, if they are around not a problem but strangers, how spiteful.

She is ready, good, time to go out it has been a long time. Slowly they were out of the door, oh she has banged the door, she is quite gentle with that, who knows what has happened to her.

Last night she was all right, all of them were quite happy, she thanked God and made him do the same for the day spent. Whatever happened this morning.

He was home the whole day, she was home as well. It must be that nasty phone, almost hate it, you can't see who you are talking to, it is disgusting, mama spends hour altogether on that thing.

She is quite annoying at times, you go on screaming and she would not listen, she talks on the phone and that is the only time she does not care for him.

Most people who come to house he is forced to greet them, awful, some poke him, some make silly remarks some make him say the rhyme, why can't the older people think of other ideas than to ask him the rhymes.

It is almost silly reciting the same thing over and over again to people you don't know.

Its quite spiteful it they asked him, holding the cheeks, no it does not hurt but how could you imagine ever liking it.

It must have been the phone for her full mood she is pushing his pram with a roughness not known to him, wait, the park is on the other side, well this part of town is full of shops, not at all bad, lots of people around.

These people are always in a hurry, rushing to get somewhere, where, don't know.

Oh she has halted, never been to this home before, he is pushed to one comer, oh he knew the other women, somehow always liked her more than the others, this one offered her what he liked, and yes it was not the rhymes with her .

Come on mama what she up to, she has started sobbing, they are talking, difficult to understand, whats wrong with her, he is supposed to cry not the other way around.

All right it's a grown up game, the other women is listening, saying things which is difficult to follow.

Stop sniffing mama she will help you, she knows how to take care, why don't you tell me, it is better.

It is a crazy moment, it does not end, mama stop it, we have to be home.

After a long time, mama is ready to leave will we go to the park now.

No, wrong turn, she is not taking him to the park why is she like that, if he screams he cries even then she would not go there, it is just like her this day, she is very angry, she is not in her best of moods.

It is really very annoying sometimes she would pamper beyond limits and now she will not even talk.

How annoying.

I have to go there with her at least the park will cheer her up, she is in good mood at the park, I always am. I scream park, park, I point finger in that direction no, she is not as much bothered to hear me today.

Well this this path is horrible, I hate it very lonely nothing to be seen.

In her anger I am pushed mercilessly and I reach home hoping now my turn of affection will come. She is not bothered today.

Now she is in the kitchen, no point screaming now she will not listen today.

I play around for some time with my toys. The toys are not keeping me happy today either. I am missing her.

Well, daddy is home earlier today, no, he has not looked at me either today, what's wrong, well after he changes he will come down to me.

No, he is not coming, she is in the kitchen, he is screaming, what are they up to, something I did, no it is not me, well, they both are screaming now something not happened ever that I know of.

Well it is unusual, she is sobbing again, oh its all right, he is kissing her, why not me, why are they like this.

In some time they come up to me, both are loving me more than they do at other times, he is offering me all goodies to eat.

They both are now watching the television well I am forced to watch it too, I hate it. They both want me to stay with that for long lonely hours.

What was the fuss earlier, I wish I could understand these adults any better.

I am to keep them happy I think, daddy is coming again my lesson, lets see what he will teach me today.

He is revising the same what we did last week. His mood is still not all right, or else he would be doing something new.

Well, my dinner time.

I have to carry on with this, she is coming towards me.

It is now late for me, I know they are awake longer than me.

But I have to be in bed, no, this is must for one, they don't ever allow anything else.

Well the day was not all that bad.

The Prophet

It was dark outside, he was on a vacation, he went out, the was alone , went out alone in the thickets.

It was amazing moonless sky with stars shimmering and the very low intensity of light was around him contributed to the carpet of darkness with enough faint hues of the surroundings.

He wandered far away from the lodge, he went on remembering his past, quite happy at thirty he had achieved everything, as much as needed.

He was not married, parents died a few years ago, not many known living acquaintances.

He was now thinking of finding a homely bride, settle with children and be happy forever.

A few furlong away from him, unknown to him the director of that magnum opus last released movie was present with his crew for his next venture.

He was going to direct a horror movie.

He was now with his special effects team, this particular scene needed an archangel advising the "hero", how to combat evil.

Everything was ready, the lasers, the sound, the night perfect for the setting.

High above in the sky hovered the archangel, in shimmering white commanding the faithful to give up worldly life, proclaim to others his prophecy, his being the chosen one.

It was a five minutes affair.

This was to change our man's life, he lay prostate, till then a practising atheist he could not believe, he was the chosen one.

He was a changed man.

Meanwhile, the director was not pleased, with the effects,it was too much of a gospel.

He stalled the plan for this particular movie.

Now it was time for our prophet to resume the task.

Gone were the worldly dreams, he was the chosen one.

In his house, which had everything was now stripped of everything, a haven for preaching.

One cannot decipher how but in a years time he had a "flock" of five hundred disciples, all were dedicated to him.

His teachings were based on the archangels teachings,he was the prophet, he would of his inner wisdom speak the "truth".

Sure enough any sane person listening to him would have gathered he spoke all the right things.

A new religion was born.

He was the prophet, it had god, archangel and his teachings, all that was needed was the holy book.

Sure enough, time passed, years rolled ,he was pleased the flock increased.

He used his common sense and prayer houses were established in every major cities.

He was nearing death, everyday he longed to meet lord god and the archangel.

They never came, he was the prophet.

All his major sermons became the holy book.

Since he had not met lord god in life, his holy book stated union with god only happens at death.

At time of his death his sole lament was the archangel had never come again.

He died.

His mausoleum stands grand in his home town, his house is a" must see" with the faithfuls.

His holy book a must.

Thousands of cities have his prayer houses.

His flock continues to rise day by day.

Meditation

A Parable from life of an Unknown prophet

Circa 2000 B.C.

He was ten and he was the chosen one, he knew that, he was tempting himself at this boyish age of the grand union. He left his parents, his friends his village for the search.

He went where no one had gone before, the wilderness was where he was to begin his search.

Practice taught him the edible which the wild offered. He was energetic and was not at all made for this mission. But he was adamant and he knew one day the grand union would happen.

He stared to think to meet the most high he needed a dwelling where peacefully he could meditate.

He stared quarrying stones, single handedly it was a near impossible task.

Knowing fully well he had a long life ahead some could be devoted in the quarry.

The stones were ready for assembly in a few years time because everyday he would think of making a larger place where the most high would meet him.

The assembly took a few years time. Once fashioned in proper place he thought of decorating the place with carvings.

Initially he thought of few carvings only. Once he started he would not be stopped, rich carvings were to touch every inch of the beautiful place he had made.

Not realizing that he was now an old man. He was occupied with the beautification of the place where the most high would be in union with him. When the work finished, age which knows but one path, showed him to doors of death.

There was was no union with most high in life. Somewhere in the thickets of wilderness is still that shrine of one man's labour whose quest for union was not met in life.

The runaway slave

*"*Eat" angrily the baked doughy bread was thrown at him.

It was his uncle, he would get that in the evening again with some vegetables and with some anger.

Uncle had erratic nature, ploughing the field, watering from the well, reaping, harvesting would make him very calm towards him, but throwing the food at him was a routine.

He had no land of his own, there never would be, uncle had three children.

He will always be their "servant"

Perhaps some clothing,that was all he would have all his life. The four, he and his cousins were today in the forest, it was reason for the hunt, a deer would be the least they will own the day.

The day was passing splendidly, pleasant, two deer had been hunted.

Lightening struck

Out of nowhere, no warning, a lion was amongst them, two ran away, his cousin was down, he went back to help him, he succeeded other ran away, he was alone with the lion.

Alas, all his strength put up for the fight was not successful in him being badly injured, somehow the lion left him alone, he lay in the forest as well.

He was sure other animal would devour him soon.

That was not to be as well.

The slave trader was passing with his "cargo" he was not pleased, probably this one would die before he reached the town.

Still, somewhere he was compassionate and god fearing he took him away with the rest.

In the seven odd days, a miracle had happened you had a renewed "him".

Indeed when the display was done a month later, he was the steal of the slave show.

He was purchased by the king's men for work in palace grounds.

Immensely respectable job.

He was full of awe for the beauty and splendour of the fortified city, the kings palace was the like of which he had never seen.

Days passed he toiled in clothes which he would had dreamed earlier, he ate food which was again a dream.

He would be rising day by day in the slave hierarchy.

He enjoyed life there.

It was not to either.

Grumbling discontent slaves had started a rebellion, slavery was monstrous, atrocity, he started getting education, he was enlightened, he was not to be a slave, the others were right.

He was among the ten who succeeded in running away, the other ten were killed trying in escape.

In a couple of days they were faraway. They knew the gaurds knew searching any would be futile.

The expenses for such a mission was far too much, probably cheaper to replace with new slaves.

The ten now were all scattered, everyone finding his haven.

He was alone, the wild provided him food, it was a long journey.

He reached a town and was looking for some job to sustain him.

At his age and no skill, he was to help the inn keeper.

The inn keeper giving him a pittance for wages kept him busy with the horses, the carriages, serving the residents of the inn, he was to help in kitchen as well.

"Eat" two baked loaves and some soup was thrown towards him would be said at every meals.

The new servant at the inn thought of it almost as an echo, but now content with the meal and rejoiced his freedom.

He hardly knew it was people like him who centuries later would abolish slavery with their wisdom.

The schizophreniac

He was thirty, he was happy with his life, yet, fate as what seemed the most miraculous of all parameters was not on his side.

He was faced with enemies who would destroy him.

Their plan was to make him mad by linking words, actions and destroy him.

He was to be made a schizophreniac.

If he was walking by the road he was shown a police van to instill fear in him.

He was to be inundated with myriad people all out to harass him.

He was put to artificial hallucinations.

His actions were assumingly linked to natural disasters, untoward happenings, all to enact hallucinating ideas in his head.

Millions were spent, his enemies were powerful.

It was too much for him.

Somehow it seemed the nations wealth was spent to destroy him.

It seemed absurd if he told anyone, still it was happening to him.

He was at his wits end.

Intelligent.

He knew what was happening.

His life was coordinated in a string of harassment.

He resorted to something very mysterious, that great unknown power.

He knew he had enemies everywhere, he was surrounded. he did what was best.

He till now knew there was no god, nothing supernatural.

Yet, he resorted to god all the same, he started penancing.

After six months it came as a miracle to him, he being faithless, yet the god of faithfuls appeared to him.

His god made a covenant with him.

From now onwards whatever he would imagine to destroy, would indeed be destroyed.

Now, he wilfully challenged his enemies.He knew enemies would have to spend time and millions to harass him, he by simply thinking could destroy them.

Everyday his enemies increased.

It became his hobby now, it became his habit now, it became his passion, he would now not rest till he had destroyed all his enemies.

If he now saw a police van,he imagined deaths,indeed death did happen.

There was no proof he was the culprit, no one could blame and catch him.

It was impossible.

If he was harassed by other means.

All he had was to think people got destroyed.

He was not to be stopped.

All he did was imagine and disaster struck.

He imagined earthquake, the quake did strike.

Thousands perished.

There was no proof against him.

Unknowingly he was turning mad.

No sane person kills.

From self defence the game had turned nihilistic.

Today when I look at him I don't know whether his enemies were wrong or he where he stands today.

The school of philosophy

He was a philanthropist, yes he was what you can call a visionary, he was immensely rich, generations of his ancestors had accumulated an untold wealth in his purse. He was no idler he was a genius when it came to money, he was not squandering spending destroying, he was accumulating as well, he had diversified in all the fields where money would not be static but be passed to his coffers. He was richest man in the world.

He had a dream a childhood dream, no amount of his business acumen, no management, education had diluted it, he was hell bent on achieving his vision, he was passionate about that dream. He wanted his favorite subject, his hobby to be shared by one and all.

He was iron willed no one could ever change his mind if he thought, he did, if he said yes, it could never be changed to a no.

He was the richest man in the world he could achieve his targets, he would achieve his targets, he had to do it.

His favorite subject was philosophy, no man on earth was present that could be regarded as a better historian of philosophers, no man could be regarded as who had better understanding of the different views in regard to this subjects in respect to geographical basis or political boundaries.

He tried to improve on that, no he was not a philosopher himself, he was busy making money, busy accumulating money. He knew to fulfill his dream he had to have more money than could be ever imagined.

He wanted his subject to be shared by one and all. His dream was colossal even by his standards they were not an easy target to achieve, yet he wanted it all the same.

He knew it he was the nidus, there would be other participants who would fulfill his dream.

He was to himself an instrument, because he was immensely rich and could provide as much as possible to achieve this unknown seemingly utopian target.

What was he to do, in principle it was easy, the world may be large but not as large as one would imagine, the world was divided but not as much as one would imagine.

He was to be the nidus beginning for a colossal project.

Friends were plenty, who said never to him, he had powerful friends, all political leader of the nation, he knew them by their first name. A man so powerful, he thought was not an impossible task to achieve what he wanted.

Yes it would have to be him. The plans were colossal almost imaginable yet he would have to begin. He was thirty five, he had a lifetime, he knew could achieve it.

An impossible target but not for him. His statistical genius knew but one way of thinking of the world, the world was one large number, simply to be thought in terms of units of thousands, millions so on and so forth.

He knew no other way for the world when the richest man has a hobby, you might say like a collector, he wanted a collection of philosophy around the world, to others it might have been impossible, but just like any other collector, he was sure he would achieve that. In his collections he would not fail.

Thus, the work started, almost the day he started things appeared easier than he thought.

His vast circle of friends, all the leaders of the world helped him on the first step, he was shocked, deeply touched, almost emotional when he came to know all the land across the world for the purpose were generously either donated by the government or were donated by his overseas friend.

He had struck victory the first round with just phone calls. There it stood all his vision were taking shape. He knew he had not paid for the land, yet he knew, none other would had succeeded in such a mission except him, his wealth was instrumental, his name was the guiding principle in such a feat, had he been a nobody the first step would never had begun.

Touched and more firm willed he became he generously donated to the overseers the sum which would see to the construction of his collections.

His name, his ambassadors, his political connections friends the world over, would make his project. Surprising he was just a nidus again, amongst much to his chagrin, the land of building, the cost was also shared by his "friends" the world over. No they would not let him do it alone.

He was to be nidus to as many, sponsors the world over would surprise him, he was to increase the number of his collection, all would be fulfilled.

His dream had become the dream of many. He was not what he was ever again. He thought in this colossal dream, the vision, he would lose it all, he would have to sacrifice with much of his wealth.

Our philanthropist knew not, he was not the only one in the world with a vision, his vision was shared by all, he has touched a large world was becoming smaller, the world where he was thinking of obstacles of barriers or great hindrance

He could see none, on the other hand, hands upon hands were joining, all to help him.

None would let him down all were busy making, he was carrying out his usual plans, not frantically running to fulfill his project. Unknown people were coordinating his work, they were all helping him make what he wanted.

He was no longer a reading philosopher he saw before his eyes the real world was it always like this, or his wealth has made it possible.

Whatever, he was the gainer, what he thought would probably take several lifetime, his life time at least would be done in years.

He would fondly not his immensely large globe with his schools, all he created, he had achieved what was seemingly an impossible task in years.

To him his subject was the mother of all others, all others a chapter of this mammoth.

Ever embracing, ever growing, providing a link to others, conveying a useful meaning of others knowledge other disciplines, knowledge had fragmented with all the speciality fields increasing, yet this mother of all subjects was the truest link.

He was not bothered of the curricula it was to be locally dictated. Yes he was a purist and wanted excellence, in his schools. He knew exactly what he wanted, yet he left the schools to do what they want,

After all his solitary wisdom could not possibly match the wisdom of millions he had involved.

To him his immensely large globe with all the dots covering and denoting his school of philosophy thrilled him and made him feel his dream have been fulfilled.

The Secret

He was sixty two, he had three children he walked with a slight limp he was as fit as one could imagine anyone his age.

It was just like another morning to him, he dressed up and from his tiny little shelter if you can call it a room descended down the stairs to the hall, he was not hurried in anything he did, he took all the time in the world for the minutest work imaginable.

Dressed he went to the office for his usual round of work, unhurried he did all the book keeping allotted to him.

The customers were thin that day, some sort of trouble had erupted in the city. He was not bothered. The newspapers never thrilled him, he had a habit of reading it very quickly as if one is simply in disgust trying to finish a deplorable job.

The work for the day continued at its pace, he went to the manager for discussion of some sort of bank loan, it seemed he was eager to help his youngest son financially for something which was troubling the young man.

For himself he simply existed on the meager, one that would help him survive.

But that was not noticed by others as they put it down to his life long habit of discipline.

Yes he got the respect of others, which was reciprocated by him.

A few good friends was all he had. His wife died few years back and he was quite unhappy for a long time.

The natural process of grieving put all his trouble to ease and he was back to himself in some time.

This day he had to find way to help his youngest son, the manager though surprised knowing his frugal habits, advanced the sum and he was with a quite content face again.

He took an early break and went out to meet the youngest son, who was quite happy to know that his current problem was solved.

The meeting was not unlike any other father and son, the son had quite a respect for the old man, the old man always condescended to the level of young man if there was anything to be conveyed.

More often than not he had parted with his savings for the three young man sometimes for no reason at all.

After this meeting, he strolled in the park with his usual limp, sitting besides the fountain for almost an hour.

This was unusual, he had not done this since his wife had died.

He was now limping back to his eldest son house.

He asked him if his son would accompany him for something he had in mind.

It was an unusual request.

With initial hesitation he accompanied his father, they were soon on the outstretch of the town.

In middle of the field was a small but, he had been there before with his father.

He was surprised, today again at this hour they were going there.

They had not talked.

On entering, the old man surprised him further by opening the floor by running a slab, it looked some sort of a celler with stairs descending.

They lit a torch, no words were exchanged, they descended the steps.

Once his eyes were adjusted to the dim vision, the eldest son saw in front of him a large, vaulted cavern, nearly quarter of a hectare.

Golden statues, golden life sized animals, chests overflowing with jewels, Gods all made of gold, gold and Jewels everywhere.

The old man took the hands of his eldest son and said in a quiet and calm voice "for four thousand years our ancestors have handed to generations upon generation this treasure, no one has used it for their survival, it is said that the keeper would realize when the right time has come to do whatever with the wealth, I had been handed similarly and have not touched anything for myself I did not think it was right time to be disclosed".

The eldest son in these two minutes knew his live would be devoted as the keeper and he knew in that moment itself he would never touch the treasure for his benefit.

Slowly they departed the place, one triumphant his keeping was successful, the other knew what was to be done in years ahead.

The three sisters

It was a sweltering hot day, he decided to go for a walk, maybe some fresh whiff of air would at least lighten his discomfort.

He went onward towards the park, somehow these few acres were a heaven of delight, tall, handsome, broad trees covered with thick coats of leaves and acres of grasses ,not to mention that large lake in the centre that added life to this whole setting was indeed an oasis in the sweltering city that seemed more like a desert now.

Sitting by the shade of the tree in the grasses,he was pondering and was wondering about his further ventures, his business had been thriving quite well. Somehow nature, fate, his fateline, positive thinking, rational approach had made it quite possible for him to reach where he was today.

He somehow knew his further expansion not be a problem.

His reverie, harsh weather, all were interrupted by three beautiful girls walking by the path by the lake, nothing extraordinary.

Yet, the pretty sight of these girls had distracted him, they were exquisitely pretty, good to look at ,most appealing.

He had an urge to acquaint himself to them.

In an attempt to acquaint to them he made his way towards the path by the lake.

No, they had not even gazed at him.

He went toward them with a piece of folded paper, that lay in his pocket.

They were surprised.

Of course it was not theirs, all the same they thanked him and proceeded.

He would not give up.

He trailed them

Somehow these girls sensed his anxiety for their acquaintance, one turned towards him and matter of factly stated she was feeling lonely in this new place, wanted to acquire new acquaintainces, that was it.

What was said hardly mattered. In a few moments they were all in the sitting room of the lovely girls.

He had nothing whatsoever in his mind, perhaps his age and his solitude made him approach them.

The conversation ranged from movies, politics, to life, in general.

It seemed they were quite educated, their approach to life was varied.

No, they too were casual talkers, with no funny intention in their mind too.

It was time to say till we meet again.

And so it was.

Next day the four were all in the same sitting room, lots of talk.

And the day next.

And the next.

It went on for a month.

Then the gentleman was on a regular visit, home was locked.

So what.

He returned the next day, and the next, the next for a month,it was to be the same.

He made enquiries with the neighbours of their whereabouts.

Surprised too, the neighbours were.

It was almost ten years, this place was locked. The owner was an old man living across the street.

On enquiry with the old man, it was learnt he did not have three daughters.

A year elapsed.

The same chance that made him meet the girls led him to an old photographer, he had an old frayed photograph of the same three girls, but the photograph was at least fifty years old.

The Trial

The impossible had happened, it never happened before convict has escaped this fortified prison, it was not a prison it was almost synonymous with the impenetrable, none in the world could compare with it, every prison in the world has a blot in its name, not this.

It was an immense search the entire region that was continuing it will be impossible for the convict to escape that was a general statement a matter of trust.

No it was not to be a second impossibility has happened 12 hours and he was not found.

He had been convicted for mass slaughter, he was twenty seven and had killed thirty people in one moment of time. He had no past history of mental defrayment and he feigned move. He admitted his guilt.

The punishment was obvious.

It was the fourth day as if by miracle he had eluded the combing operation of area in progress and was now a hundred kilometers away from that dreaded place.

He saw amongst the wilderness a lonely dwelling, he was sure it was deserted, the appearance suggestive of much.

The door was open, he entered surprisingly it was a livable home, someone came down the stairs a man of forty broad, muscular and strong, he had a revolver in his hand. There was no mistake from appearance what this young man had done.

The master of the house placed the weapon on the table and asked him to enter.

After changing his attire and refreshment they were sitting in the crumbling but livable room.

"I am no judge yet I ask you what you have done". The young man was mesmerized by the unwanted welcome he had recieved, the very calmness of the master of the house. He knew it was his duty to explain himself to this party.

The conversation which ensued explained that the master of the house was a lovely person, retired to this part in pursuit of his hobby of botany, he visits the nearest town only on pretext of supplying himself of the necessities of life. An orphan knew not anyone else in the world nor cared to know anyone but himself. An occasional friend would be invited here that too a rarity.

This young man gathered courage and knew he was in right company, law takes its course, the master of the house cared not for the law neither was bothered to assist it in any form. He had a duty towards law was not known to this gentleman.

The young man explained his crime of killing thirty people in a moment of time in a gathering in the auditorium. When they were all enjoying music, but that was not to be in their fate.

Law abiding or not the master of the house was quite alarmed and asked for further explanation.

This young man was a qualified architect upto twenty six, he knew not of anything of law or crime in any way as most other people do not know when they will come across its path.

It happened this year he got nearer to the separatist party which existed in the state, their ideologies were appealing to him.

In the next logical step that came to him, was that he joined the hard core terrorist group, whose existence is a secret, their mission, anarchy, chaos, to destabilize the state in an attempt to assist the separatist party to achieve its goal.

This seasoned gentleman, was aloof, yet he knew the world, he knew how these things are worldwide, young people are coaxed or like this young lad with their enthusiasm enter such a group with almost a missionary zeal.

There was no debate, some with zeal hidden in themselves go to the extreme step of terrorist activities.

Here was a young man, normal in all respect, qualified, calm with surrounding, not insane yet this improbable mission he had executed with no thoughts of repentence.

The master asked would he do it again. The answer was yes, he had devoted his life to the mission, if he was not caught he would lead his job as an architect quite normally.

Now he had no choice but to carry on with his mission and do thing else.

The elder was debating himself, what is a nation, a group of ethnic diverse people, what is separatist, one who carves a nation out of the nation, who is a terrorist one assisting the separatist.

He knew no law, cared for none, he could only pacify himself of diversity creating such animosities.

Dissatisfaction gives birth to these monstrosities. To this elder there was no solution.

Had he been a judge, what verdict would he give, for murder death yes, what if he is a freedom fighter. He let the young man go with no compulsion. Later he sat and thanked himself that he is not a judge.

The Unfinished Painting

He was painter, not a great master we know of. No he was not the small sized, poverty stricken, eccentric, sedentary type. He was broad shouldered, the face gleamed with aristocracy, very strong, powerful limbs, he was not a professional, his tyre company the brand a household name in all parts of the world. He was very very rich yet his hobby of painting made him know to himself that he was a painter,that was all he said. Tyres bring me money, what is my contribution he said. My contribution to myself.

He made immensely lovely paintings, yet he would never say they could be contribution to society. He never had his work exhibited to the world.

Not even his family and his intimate friends knew they existed, to him and him alone he was "the Painter". His mansion 20 km south of the airport was as lavish as one could imagine.

One large room served him his studio, he had all his canvases there, he could had easily made an art gallery in the mansion or he could had a private run art gallery all at his own expense.

But honestly it never occurred in his mind. No the astonishing part is he did not even consider mounting his canvas on frames. They were all as such.

It was this oddity which even he could not explain. Why if not for others to see surely one mounts them for one's own delight.

But he will not have it. It was his little secret. He had finished his 68th canvas and was starting on the next, he was thirty five, he was sure himself if he had his works exhibited none would go unnoticed.

For his next he had promised himself a master piece, he was feeling confident, he did not believe hundred percent inspiration made a master piece, it was hundred percent confidence he thought could make his masterpiece.

For his project he was thinking of a portrait, this portrait would be the best, legend,forever. He wanted to immortalize, he had the faith his next work would be immortal.

He was now at it, searching his model, he placed number of advertisements, he went to all the right places to find his face. He roamed the city and tried to see the occasional passerby. He knew exactly in his mind what he was searching for. As if his mathematical genius, taught him the exact face he was looking for. He had yet to match with the real person. He was not alarmed, almost a month had passed. He was confident he would find that face, soon very soon. His business like attitude to life has taught him he would soon spot her.

Then he went to the town next, he took a long vacation to the surprise of all he was surrounded with, he went to the town next and then next and the next it went on he was tired now he was returning home.

He was now a little less confident than earlier but in a show of his endeavour to excel he was now going back but not without trying.

He was a thousand km from his house he decided to walk, lovely the countryside en route.

Time passed in his pace, slow but definitely, he was neither in a hurry to reach home or not worried if he was still not there, village after village he was passing. He had a hope he will just see her.

Somehow destiny works in the direction of the assumer. Finally the very roadside where he was walking not few yards away from the curve of a path came out a young girl, very very much what he wanted there was no parameters which did not match her with her imagination, it was her, the very same picture.

His dealings with thousands of people over the year rich and poor, eminent and powerless, had made high so confident that he thought all he would do is go back home with her. There was no doubt about this package not going along with her back home.

He finally went up to her and exactly told the purpose summarizing it and neatly describing all he had to in few minutes and in an uninterrupted stream of remarks asked if she would go back along with him.

"Yes" said the girl. He was neither surprised nor happy he had assumed such.

Way back the girl in the similar way of expressive tone gave all her introduction. Summary she was there on a restive vacation, surprising she worked in the same city as he was in, as a photographer, she had never ever given a thought that one day she would model at the other end. No she was single and had but distant relations to speak of with whom much contact there never was or ever would be.

Time flew they reached home, after the usual routine, he was now all full and back at his studio with her.

The girl insisted on asking his work, no one has asked before, no one knew they existed. In an almost renewed him, he took out all and opened out everything in the floor, it was afternoon, the girl went from me to next and again to the first and next, no words were exchanged, he out in the corner and she went on looking at them all and it was morning, he had no words to speak of, she would not speak. There was now in this broad shouldered majestic youth a heart which he knew not had existed ,an emotion he knew not would ever come to this thirty five year old, he was in love, what else could it be now his model and the studio and the paintings and the undone paintings and the rest of his possessions.

It was this twelve hours of his life which was like twelve years, it went on in an unending succession of range of emotions, he forgot he was the painter, he was only with that girl, he wanted to just sit in front of her, the painting that would be there would just not occur in his head, he was nowhere where he had been, it was a different experience.

She on the other hand was running from one to the other, she was no patron of art, neither a painter nor a critic, she was not one who you would say an authority. Yet she was how all with him, his works had an air of him, she could physically feel his presence by his works, it was an unusual experience, she was now a part of his works a part of him she would be as a model to be immortalized, yet now already she was a part of him. It was similar with her the love for that man evident eyeing him once in these long hours had already made her a part of him.

From time to time she wanted to kiss him, embrace him she wanted to be physically touched by him. It was an unending passion which arose from a gentle calm to the frenzied storm, what was she to do, no she was not the modest type. She was not ashamed to embrace him right this instant.

She was just hoping how he was feeling, the journey had not conveyed any feelings how he felt for her, if at all very old approach towards her.

The next day the whole usual routine were to continue for the day, they had not shared any of their feelings, with not exchange of feelings the day perhaps had mellowed the initial frenzy, in the evening when they met in the studio it was with no canvases to hinder or create a barrier for their feelings.

The work took precedence, that was to start first, it was not the feelings were not there but he in his show of pretent to his feeling suppressed them and she in her misunderstanding of his exterior self went on until the job they were in, strokes of the brushes would be scarce each day he wanted to prolong her stay in front of her, she was also not in a hurry. She wanted this to last forever.

The stroke became scarce and scarce, he took a long leave from his place of work. The studio it was to be running, afternoon, night with shorter and shorter breaks, finally, there were no breaks at all a continous stretch of time with strokes becoming practically none.

She was filled with a feeling of joy not even known to her, she was becoming emaciated, he was becoming emaciated, both were now feeble, extremely at that.

He was also now fatigued, he knew his end was coming, he realized that her end was near as well. Both have never spoken a word, he saw the canvas it was very far from complete, he now had the urge to finish it, he frenzied to do that.

But the realization had been extremely late, very late it would never finish with best of his intention.

Her smile had never vanished, she would die smiling for him, he is to be helped in finishing his work.

She saw him leave the brush he was walking towards the store of his canvases, without her realizing he set flames to the entire store, she was with her smile waiting for his return to the brush.

He limped back to the canvas, the others were to burn, this would have to survive. It was impossible, he sat on the high stool to finish.

When it happened with the tired hands the strokes became almost none. He was now left without the spirit of life. She was also gone without the spirit of life.

The life of the other paintings had vanished in flames. There was an eerie silence with no moment neither of the woman nor the man, nor the life of the canvas exuded any life.

Yes, when they were found only life in that room was the unfinished painting.

His family left the mansion, it was to be a museum.

The sole surviving painting can still be seen in the studio if you happen to pass by the city.

Wanted

❝........... to be hanged till death."

The accusation proved without doubt, sentence pronounced, he was aware of the consequences.

The travel to the prison, a two hour long drive from the court room changed it all.

Human mind knows no restraint, knows no written law of man, neither can it be imprisoned.

What happened was unknown, in these two hours he was not in same senses anymore, he had a total loss of memory, who he was.

How, it cannot be explained, the sentence of death has probably done something.

He was now completely unaware of the surroundings, the guards pushed him to the allotted cell.

They have perceived nothing.

No one exactly rejoices at the death sentence, his complete silence was nothing unfamiliar or thought provoking.

When it happened, how it happened again it cannot be explained, he was somewhat successful in escape from prison to the world outside.

He had forgotten the mass massacre he had done a year ago, the courts of law, the police had not.

He was the "most wanted" criminal in this year's proceedings.

He was neither behaving insanely, nor was he being perceived as one.

It was complete amnesia

He proceeded from start to another and continued with neither a past or a future.

Sitting under a tree, he overheard passerby's conversation, they were discussing someone with some details.

He assumed it was him.

From now on that was to be his name, he found himself a suitable job in the many industries that abound a large city.

No one suspected or bothered him.

With the loss of his memory and new identity it was miraculous, his face had changed to a remarkable extent, and the hair do in the new style completely failed to reveal himself to the world as the same "wanted" whose poster was surprisingly at the factory gates as well where he worked.

He was content, in due time his fabricated stories would make up his character, if people discussed his origin he would fake something.

If it was his parents, he would be an orphan friends.

No, a new comer in search of opening in the great city.

No one was surprised.

He was not conscious though of what he was doing, it was simply a reflex.

With passing year the search had waved to minimum intensity.

of late some victims of the massacre. Who worked here were remembering that episode with much vehemence.

He joined the conversation and no one could but admire him for the way he was condemning the dastardly act, he was simply shocked at such a happening.

Moreover some victims who have survived were amongst his best friends.

He was often invited to their house for some pretext or the other.

This new life was entirely devoted to his new surroundings – Mentally he was at peace with himself.

His stories had convinced himself. He was not ever bothered as to their truth.

To him it was the truth.

Years passed, in his new identity he was successful, happy, content and as normal as any person could possibly be.

Life was extremely kind to him.

His bliss culminated when with marriage he was proud father of two.

Years would roll by and his life continued to prosper.

Such is sometimes the "truth of life."

The Enemy of the state

There is no anarchist worse than the patriot if he revolts.

It is common knowledge the closer you examine a painting more flaw it reflects than the beauty.

Why only the state in its closeness anything you value ideas, religion, patriotism, family, just about anything. When you value something dearly, your mental image is a distorted version of the reality, you want perfection, nothing in the world really is. It can never be.

This tale is perhaps more reflection of such an idea.

Growing in a secular environment, patriotism was fundamental in his thinking of other abstracts, his success, family's success and the nation were all linked in a mesh of his ideas.

Well, he was young, he did not hate an idea of united world yet a sense of belonging, national pride was part of his character.

For studies he went abroad, the stay of four years was unknown to him to have an immense impact on his life.

On entering, the very strangeness of the most familiar was very disturbing.

After two years of his return the contrast which is obvious for a developing nation to have with the G-7 turned his feelings to almost hatred.

It was not natural, it was his setback. He had a vision of a different place, the familiar was very much against his wishes.

To live forever in such a static society somewhat disturbed him completely. Almost a complete hatred in his mind ensued.

People spend their lives with this contrast; his very sensitive mind was extremely disturbed.

With no positive thinking and no foreseeable remedy he turned against the system.

He left all his precious work. Unemployed he knew he was committing suicide, he knew the outcome. Yet he was to destroy this place.

It was not difficult for him to conceive a plan of action.

He poisoned the water supply, thousands died.

How he was successful is difficult to imagine yet he did.

The city lots innumerable lives.

He was "most wanted".

The entire nation's police at their heels to catch the culprit. It was unimaginable massive combing operation in the country.

With provision for three months, only fit for survival he knew he would be found one day, he hid himself in one of the large industrial warehouses which remain locked for years. He somehow managed to be inside.

He would come out after months.

The combing operation continued.

He will be found one day, the nation had vowed with a vengeance to punish him.

The national pride was hurt.

Their incompetence was shamed by the entire world.

The country was mocked and lambasted internationally. The combing operation was endless, ceaseless, the nation would not rest till the culprit was found.

He emerged only to buy provisions for months. Months turned into years.

He knew the operation was ceaseless.

He did not give up either.

Pigeoned in a corner he was helpless, he was turning weak every day on such living.

The endless search continued and he became frail, then look to all sorts of illness, finally he was no more.

At his death, he kept on admiring the wonderful job executed and was happy in destroying the nation's pride.

Years later the Skelton with leftover provisions were amongst the seized, unexplained by the police.

The poisoning case is still open to investigation.

The mad man

It was now almost thousand years, god had said the age of prophets were gone.

No more would come.

Tha faithfuls knew that.

But it has been signed by god himself, no more prophets.

He was a pious, faithful person, did all by the law, lived by the commandments.

What god saw in him, no one can say.

God decided to send his archangel to the faithfuls again, this time very unlike to his previous diktat, he had changed his mind.

God sent archangel to him he was to start a new religion, a new holy book, and all necessary to gods plan ,he was to continue the same.

Of course, the archangel had to come every now and then, to make him a prophet and polish him to be the chosen one.

The first time the faithful saw it was difficult for him to believe, the archangel conveyed gods great design.

What else can be done "proclaim", said gods angel.

So it was, he started with his neighbours, they were his best friends till now.

Now, the revolt.

He was at first beaten and then thrown into police custody.

Archangel was in the prison too.

Bad for him, now he was beaten up by the police. He was now in a lunatic asylum

God's grand design did not end there.

He was now beaten up by the lunatics as well.

Thrown out of the hospital as well, he roamed the wilderness, god continued and went on sending the archangel.

He was at his wits end, he could not coax the occasional traveller to his religion, because they would beat him up, spit on him.

It was a sad plight for him.

He lived upto eighty, died in the wilderness, not a single faithful.

He had memorised the teachings given by the archangel, no holy book could be written, there was no one to write the book.

No prayer houses of the new religion came to be founded.

He had failed archangel.

Archangel failed god.

God failed his faithfuls in the new design.

9 788194 804109